BIG JACK SLOAN'S RIDERS EMERGED FROM THE TREES WITH THEIR GUNS DRAWN, SPURRING THEIR HORSES.

Ready for the ambush, Lassiter stood up and braced himself on the bench of the stagecoach. He aimed his rifle at the first rider and fired. The thief pitched backward from the saddle. Sloan yelled at the others to keep going.

Lassiter levered another round into the barrel and fired. Again there was a sharp crack and the rider toppled sideways. Lassiter got his rifle ready again and noticed the kid—a youngster on his way to join the Army—getting out of the stagecoach.

"Stay inside!" Lassiter yelled down at him.

"I ain't letting you get all of them yourself," the kid yelled back. He pulled his big Colt and began fanning it wildly in the direction of Sloan and the gang.

Lead thumped into the wood of the stage and one bullet sang off the iron railing at Lassiter's feet. The kid spun into the first volley and fell, leaving a wide smear of blood against the stage door.

As the stagecoach driver fought to control the horses, Lassit_____ _____ __ __ ground and dropped to one l_____ getting set behin____

D0956889

Other *Leisure* books by Loren Zane Grey:

THE LASSITER LUCK
LASSITER TOUGH
LASSITER GOLD
A GRAVE FOR LASSITER
AMBUSH FOR LASSITER
LASSITER

LASSITER'S RIDE

Loren Zane Grey

LEISURE BOOKS NEW YORK CITY

A LEISURE BOOK®

October 2008

Published by special arrangement with Golden West Literary Agency.

Dorchester Publishing Co., Inc.
200 Madison Avenue
New York, NY 10016

ISBN 10: 0-8439-5818-9
ISBN 13: 978-0-8439-5818-8

Printed in the United States of America.

10 9 8 7 6 5 4 3 2

Visit us on the web at www.dorchesterpub.com.

LASSITER'S RIDE

1

THE WEATHERED WOODEN SIGN told Lassiter he had eight miles of mountain trails left before he hit Glitter Creek, Idaho Territory. Coeur d'Alene lay behind him and the gold fields of Montana Territory a ways yet to the east. He was in the middle of untamed country.

The tall gunfighter lifted himself in the saddle to stretch; it had been a long ride up the West Coast from California. His reputation had managed to follow him there, and after a long shootout in a Sacramento saloon, he had found himself riding away from a run-in with authorities who just wouldn't understand.

As he rode along the trail he thought of the many towns he had been to and the country he had traveled over the years—none of it without trouble. He hoped the people up here this far north might not have heard of him. It would make his time spent here that much easier.

As he read the sign, Lassiter was aware of five riders who had just appeared at the crest of a hill. They were sitting their horses and watching him, pointing and talking among themselves. Maybe it was his dress, the black leather chaps and the low-slung, black-handled .44 pistols that clung to the outside of each leg, but people would stop to wonder about him, knowing instinctively he was someone strong in a hard land. He was a man with a trademark, this man they called Lassiter; and it didn't matter where he went, people had a way of knowing him.

The riders remained atop the hill, studying Lassiter from afar. It was as if they were making a decision whether or not to come down. Lassiter subtly made sure he could draw his .44 Winchester from the scabbard easily. He already knew his twin Colts were loaded and ready. He paid the riders no real attention, and after a time they turned their horses and rode into the timber out of sight.

Call it experience or maybe a gunfighter's intuition, but Lassiter suddenly felt that same old sixth sense: trouble wasn't far off. The more he thought about it, the more he was sure the riders he had just seen along the high ridge above the trail were looking for some easy pickings of some kind.

Money and people who were carrying it was what the riders were looking for, Lassiter was certain. It was the start of a busy time up here in Idaho Territory now that summer had come to the mountains. That meant a considerable increase in traffic on the Mullen Road, the main link between the booming gold fields here in the mountains and the growing cities along the coast.

There was an element here that preyed on travelers. They preferred to call themselves road agents instead of thieves. Either way the results were the same. People with gold watches and bulging purses usually lost them along this trail. A good road agent could get wealthy in just a few months.

Lassiter had been studying a newspaper clipping off and on since leaving Coeur d'Alene. He once again took the clipping from his vest pocket and read the ad for a shotgun rider on the Glitter Creek Stage Lines. Someone who was not easily intimidated was needed to help guard the stage as it went from Glitter Creek to points west toward Coeur d'Alene.

What the article actually meant was that a man who could use a gun well was needed. The Glitter Creek Stage Lines had likely fallen victim to road agents. Lassiter was down on his spending money, and he figured the position would pay a man like him quite well. He hoped the position was still open.

He had just gotten the clipping tucked away when he heard shooting not far from him. It sounded as if it was coming from just up the trail, along the ridge where the five riders had disappeared not long before. It appeared they had already found somebody to rob.

Lassiter kicked his horse into a full gallop and covered a good distance without hearing any more gunfire. The pines on each side of the trail were a green blur as his big roan surged ahead, Lassiter holding a .44 in his right hand.

Lassiter rode over a small ridge right into the on-coming rush of the five road agents. The third one in line was carrying a woman on his saddle in front of him. She was dressed in black gingham and was kicking and screaming, trying to break his tight hold around her middle. She had dark red hair that was coming loose from under her veiled hat.

The first two road agents opened fire on Lassiter. One of them had a Winchester and was shooting wild.

Lassiter heard the wind whoosh out of his roan's chest as a bullet tore into the horse above its left shoulder. Lassiter managed to jump free as the big horse went down in the middle of the trail.

After rolling to break the fall, Lassiter regained his feet and opened fire. The two front riders were now bearing down on him and he fanned his .44, knocking them both from their saddles. Lassiter shot once again as the other three tried to turn their horses from his line of fire. He could see that he had hit the thief who held the woman.

The thief yelled and released the woman. He grabbed his neck with one hand and jerked his horse's reins sideways with his other hand. The horse stumbled, and the woman in black gingham screamed as she was thrown off.

The two remaining road agents were spurring their horses, one of them leaning sideways in the saddle as he rode, his hands clenching the saddle horn to stay on. He appeared to be quite young—too young to die from a bullet through the middle. He had been hit badly and was hanging on to his horse with a sheer act of will. He couldn't last long.

Lassiter turned his concentration to the thief who had been holding the woman. His horse was now on its feet, trotting away, and he was coming to his hands and knees, swearing. A bullet had grazed his neck and there was a wide line of flowing red that trailed down onto his shirt.

The thief was moving with difficulty. He seemed to have one crippled leg, a leg which appeared shorter than the other one. But he was enraged and it didn't seem to slow him. He was rising with a .45 in his right hand.

Lassiter pulled his second .44 revolver, holding it in his left hand. There was one shot left in the revolver he held in his right hand. Looking down the bores of two pistols, it would have seemed that the thief would see his odds were nothing. But he was determined and crazed. Lassiter eased the hammers back on both guns and held down on the man, warning him.

"Just let that forty-five of yours drop in front of you."

Lassiter knew immediately his words were wasted. The road agent answered only with his eyes, a defiant squint, and continued up with the pistol, cocking it as he charged. Lassiter let go with both revolvers and blue smoke filled the air. A series of neat round holes appeared in the man's shirt above his heart. He toppled forward and lay still.

With deft and nimble fingers, Lassiter reloaded his pistols quickly, watching for the return of the other two riders. But all was still along the forest road except the woman in the black gingham dress. She was groaning, trying to get to her feet.

Lassiter went over to her and had her lie back down for a moment until she could recover from her fall. She was a very pretty woman, even soiled and disheveled as she was. Though she was pale and disoriented, it was still apparent that she was a woman of class and means. Otherwise, she appeared not to be so much hurt as badly shaken.

When he saw that the woman was settled some, Lassiter went to his fallen horse and untangled a canteen of water from the saddle horn. The roan's breathing was ragged and it sickened Lassiter to hear it. His good horse was dying slowly from the chest wound. Lassiter pointed the barrel of his .44 behind the animal's ear, then turned away as he pulled the trigger. The horse jerked once and lay still.

Lassiter lingered for a time near the horse, looking sadly at the roan's half-closed eyes. The animal had been his for a couple of years now, strong and reliable, and had brought him through a lot of rough times and rough country. It was hard to lose a good horse like that. It made him want to take the crippled robber's horse and chase down the other two and finish them. But there was the woman to think about now.

When Lassiter returned to her, she was sitting up against the trunk of a pine. Her hands were busy with her red hair, tucking it back beneath her hat as best she could, watching Lassiter from the corners of her eyes. The color had returned to her face and she seemed embarrassed. She took a drink of water from Lassiter's canteen and thanked him.

"I'm sorry about your horse," she said. "I will have my father give you another one."

"It will be hard to replace him," Lassiter said, looking back to where the roan lay still. "But you certainly don't have to blame yourself."

"Just the same," the woman said, "I want you to know I'll make it right by you. I'd like to. You just saved me from those robbers. My father owns the stage lines. He has plenty of horses."

Lassiter took the newspaper clipping from his pocket. "Harold Mitchell is your father?"

She nodded. "I'm Lanna Mitchell." She was doing her best to smooth her black gingham dress, cleaning bits of trail mud off with her fingers. "I was just on my way into Glitter Creek from San Francisco when those robbers showed up on the trail. There was no trouble at all until we got to this ridge."

"I was hoping to get a job as shotgun rider on your father's stage line," Lassiter said. "Was there a rider on this stage?"

"Yes, there was," Lanna answered, "but he's dead now." Her look was faraway. She seemed to be reflecting on the incident that had just occurred, sorting it through her mind as if to decide if it had all been real.

Lassiter watched her. He reached out and took her hand in his and squeezed it gently. She didn't pull away from him.

"It's all right. Get rid of it," he said. "Get it out of your mind so you won't have to think about it again."

Lanna was silent, the tears coming again. She kept the faraway look, reliving what had happened. Finally she shrugged. "They just shot everybody, whether they had their hands up or not. Then they took me. I have to thank you."

She began to cry and Lassiter gave her his shoulder, letting her get it out of her system. It was best this way—she would not hold it deep within to cause trauma later.

When she had composed herself, she dabbed at her eyes once again and looked away, apologizing for having used his shoulder to cry on.

"Nothing to be sorry about, ma'am," Lassiter told her. "You've had a bad day to say the least. How are you feeling now?"

"Much better, thank you. What do we do now?"

"We had better get down out of here right away," Lassiter answered. "They might be back for their dead buddies. We don't want to be here then."

Lassiter took the saddle from his dead roan and placed it back in the trees off the trail. No one would see it, and he could return for it another time. He took the Winchester from its scabbard and laid it down by Lanna.

"Can you shoot that?" he asked.

Lanna looked up at him. Her expression was hard. "I sure can," she said. "I'll shoot them if they come back. I'll shoot all of them."

"I'm going over the hill to see what's left of the stage and the passengers. What do you want to do?"

"I don't want to go with you," Lanna said. "I don't want to see what's over there again."

"I didn't figure you would," Lassiter said. "That's why I'm leaving the rifle with you. Anybody comes and you shoot once into the air. If they don't stop before I get back, turn the barrel on them. Understand?"

Lanna nodded and Lassiter walked the short distance to where the road agents had held up the stage. The horses stood in harness, waiting for someone to urge them forward. Two male passengers lay still on their backs next to the front wheels, their lifeless eyes staring into the blue sky overhead. The driver hung over the railing and the shotgun rider was on the ground on the other side of the stagecoach, curled in a ball where he had died of massive stomach wounds. Likely the thief with the Winchester had opened fire on his midsection.

The brake was still set on the stage, so the horses would go nowhere until someone got up on the platform. Lassiter thought it better just to let them go and leave the stage for the time being. There was little here now that was worth saving.

The team was restless from the blood smell but did not panic when Lassiter approached and let them out of harness. They began to trot down the road toward Glitter Creek and Lassiter knew they would be down in town before too much time passed, alerting everyone to trouble up on the ridge.

Lassiter then dragged the bodies of the fallen men from the stagecoach off the trail. They would have to be taken down into town and buried; but that would have to wait. Getting Lanna out of here and to her father was the priority now.

When he returned to where Lanna was sitting under the tree, he noticed she had been crying again. The tears had been effectively wiped away, but the redness in her blue eyes couldn't be disguised. She was really upset over what had happened at the stage.

"I just hope my father doesn't become too worried," she said. "He's bound to wonder when the horses you released go down into town."

"We'll get down there as soon as we possibly can," Lassiter said. "I just need to decide how these road agents might be thinking. I don't know this territory and I don't know where they came from. If their hideout is nearby, that could be important to our getting out of here."

"I don't know anything about this area, either," Lanna said. "This is my first trip out here."

She seemed to be in a heavy daze, and it occurred to Lassiter that shock might be setting in. The day was warm and he didn't think covering her would help. He gave her more water and had her lie down for a short while.

"I feel much better now," she finally said. "I'm ready to go whenever you are."

"We'll get ourselves one of the horses they left

behind," Lassiter told Lanna. "Do you feel like you can ride through some rough country?"

Lanna nodded. "I can do whatever has to be done."

Lassiter was glad to hear that. Luckily she was a spunky one, and time was an important factor now. Lassiter knew if he and Lanna didn't get going soon, the road agents might return. They hadn't expected him before, but if they returned, they would be after blood.

2

LASSITER REMEMBERED THE CRIPPLED road agent who had been carrying Lanna on his horse. The horse was a big sorrel, and Lassiter found it grazing peacefully in a little meadow just off the road. It was a good horse, young and stocky and good for mountain riding. Lassiter just hoped it would take both of them on its back at once.

With its size, Lassiter figured the sorrel must be used to having people ride double on occasion. Some horses weren't fond of carrying two riders, and Lassiter knew they couldn't take a chance with a horse that wasn't able to hold them both. Fortunately, the sorrel remained by them as some of the other horses seemed to have strayed off quite a distance.

Lassiter caught the sorrel and talked to it a while before he led it over to Lanna. He helped her onto the back of the horse and waited for a reaction. There was none; the sorrel must have been used to having someone on behind and didn't mind that she had her feet against his flanks.

Lassiter then climbed on, and the two of them rode into the timber off the main trail. It would be better, Lassiter decided, to take a little longer getting to Glitter Creek on the back trails than it would taking a chance on meeting more road agents on the main road.

Lassiter let the big sorrel take its time in negotiating the steep trails up and down the mountains toward Glitter Creek. It was rough and he could feel Lanna bouncing around behind him, trying to hold back her groans as the saddle squeaked under their weight. The ups and downs were a strain and Lassiter hoped that Lanna wouldn't want to stop.

But Lanna had road agents on her mind just as much as he did.

"I wonder if we're going to run into more of them," Lanna thought out loud. She was riding behind Lassiter with her hands holding the saddlebags, gritting her teeth against the rough leather beneath her. She had thought of putting her arms around Lassiter for support, but had decided not to do that.

"Thieves wouldn't expect to make much by traveling the back trails like this," Lassiter assured her. "The main road is where the profit is."

"Are you sure?" Lanna asked.

"Would you take this trail if you knew there was an easier way?" Lassiter asked her. "Think how your bottom feels right now."

For the first time he heard Lanna laugh.

Though it was just a little one, it showed she was beginning to relax.

"Not on your life," she answered. She was hanging on to the saddle in good fashion for as rough as the trail was, taking her jolts without complaint. "You know who I am,'' she finally said. "But I don't know who you are."

"My name is Lassiter."

"Just Lassiter?"

"Just Lassiter. I don't come from any place in particular, and I'm really not headed anywhere, either. I need a job for a time, and I saw your father's ad in a paper in Coeur d'Alene."

"Judging from what I just saw, you could sure do the job," Lanna said. "Where did you learn to shoot like that?"

"It's taken a long time."

"If I didn't know better, I would be more afraid of you than the robbers who held up the stage. From a distance you look like the wrath of God."

"I don't intend to be," Lassiter assured her, "but my dress is for good reason."

Lanna was quiet for a time, thinking. She adjusted herself on the saddle behind Lassiter and cleared her throat.

"I have never been out so far from the city before, and I don't know this country," she said, "but it seems to me that you're the type of man the newspapers contain stories about. Are you a gunfighter or something?"

Lassiter thought a moment before he answered. "I once chose to use guns to settle a problem. I settled the problem, and I've been using the guns ever since."

"I'm not sure I really understand what you're telling me," Lanna said.

"I said I was better than the next man in a gunfight once, and I'm still living up to that," Lassiter said. "I don't look for trouble, but it sure finds me. All I want is a few dollars and a little comfort to live on. But people don't want to afford you something if they can take it away from you."

"Is it the land that makes the people out here so wild?" Lanna asked. "The land is so rugged. Is that why the people are like they are?"

"There's not many comforts out here," Lassiter said. "People have to take comfort in one another."

"This is much different from what I'm used to," Lanna said. "I've been in the city most of my life, sheltered and happy. I've known nothing but comfort and courtesy, apart from all that existed outside of the estate. I saw things, but I've never had to live with them. Now that my mother has died and my father's wealth depends on what happens to him out in this savage country, I will have to learn about what happens outside of high walls. I guess I will learn what you are telling me soon enough."

Lassiter did not want to pry into Lanna's personal affairs, nor those of her father, but it occurred to him that the financial circumstances of Harold Mitchell were somehow in jeopardy. For some reason he had staked his future on the whims of the frontier gold fields. It could make him a lot richer, or leave him penniless. At the worst end of it all, it might also leave him dead.

"From what I've seen of you so far," Lassiter finally told Lanna, "you will go a long way in helping your father out. It will take a lot to keep you down. It would be hard for anybody to get their first feel of this country by watching people die and then barely escape being kidnapped on top of it all. You seem to be taking it all much better than a person would expect."

"I appreciate your kind words, Mr. Lassiter," Lanna said. "But I have yet to get over what happened today. In fact, I am quite certain I shall never get over it. You see, I was engaged to marry one of the men who was killed.''

It was Lassiter's turn to be stunned. There was no way he could have guessed as much. He could hear Lanna crying behind him again. After a time she regained her composure.

''My father did not know of this,'' Lanna continued. ''Under the circumstances, I would prefer that he never learn of it. He will have enough to contend with as it is. I should not have even mentioned it to you. But for some reason I did. Now I am hoping you will forget this conversation. Could you grant me that courtesy, Mr. Lassiter?''

''I could, ma'am,'' Lassiter said. ''Your business is your own.''

They crossed a small creek, Glitter Creek, from which the town took its name, and Lassiter held the horse for a time to study the main road up and down. Lanna was uncomfortable but patient. She realized that this dark stranger was a professional at staying alive in this savage land. Finally, when he urged the horse out onto the road to cover the last few miles into town, she took a deep breath.

Lassiter rode into the town of Glitter Creek with Lanna on behind him and watched the people gather along the street. They stared hard at him, some backing up and others merely watching him closely. There weren't many men who came into this part of the country who looked so formidable, with black chaps and twin Colts.

As they rode through the middle of town, Lassiter noticed that the horses from the stage were standing in front of a hotel named after the town. A lot of people were gathered there. Lassiter could see that besides noticing him, they were noticing Lanna as well. One of them ran into the hotel, and in a moment a well-dressed man came out and hurried into the street.

"That's my father," Lanna told Lassiter. "He looks to be nearly crazy with worry."

Lanna jumped down from the horse and went into her father's arms. He was of medium height and his hair was of the same hue as his daughter's. He looked to be of the kind that could be firm yet polite. But Lanna was right; at this moment he looked terribly strained.

Lassiter got down from the sorrel and tied it to a railing. Harold Mitchell held Lanna for a time, asking her if she was all right and wondering who Lassiter was.

"He saved my life, Father," Lanna said. "Road agents held up the stage and killed everyone but me." Her eyes brimmed with tears once again, thinking of her lost fiancé. "The thieves just shot everyone and tried to take me with them. If Mr. Lassiter hadn't come along, I don't know what would have happened. I guess I'd be sitting in some cabin hideout somewhere in the mountains with those terrible men."

Harold Mitchell was watching Lassiter. The shock of what had happened was still evident in his face, as well as the realization that Lassiter had come along just in time or both his daughter and he would be facing very difficult circumstances.

"I don't know how to thank you," Harold Mitchell told Lassiter, taking his hand and shaking it. "I'm Harold Mitchell and you are my guest here for as long as you wish."

Lassiter nodded. "I appreciate that. How often does your stage get the kind of treatment afforded it today?"

"All too often," Mitchell commented. "I'm having trouble keeping the line open at all. People are hearing about the problems and just aren't coming to Glitter Creek."

Lassiter took a piece of paper from inside his vest—the newspaper ad he had carried with him from Coeur d'Alene.

"I was hoping I might go to work for you," he said, handing the ad to Mitchell. "The reason I came here is to answer your request for a shotgun rider on the stage."

Mitchell's eyebrows raised. "I see, well that is a coincidence. I was about to bring that very subject up to you, Mr. Lassiter. I can't imagine anybody more suitable for the position. Of course, you realize the job is certainly not without its perils."

"I would expect that, Mr. Mitchell," Lassiter said. "It occurs to me that this whole territory might be suffering a great deal from the likes of the men who held up the stage today. Do you have any idea who these thieves are?"

Mitchell nodded. "There is an outlaw stronghold not far out of town, just over the mountain from the Mullen Road. They hang out in a cabin in Miner Canyon. Their leader is a big man named Jack Sloan. He and his bunch have already accounted for three shotgun riders in the last year."

"I believe their streak will end there," Lassiter said with confidence. "They say the third time is a charm. I like to say that when you try the fourth time, your luck has gone completely under."

Mitchell smiled. "I like your attitude, Mr. Lassiter, yes, I do. I can see that things will be changing around here. My worry now is for the men who have gone out to see what happened to the stage. Some of them are pretty young, and I'm afraid they don't know what they're getting themselves into."

Some of the men were already coming back into town. There were three who rode in, one sitting in the saddle awkwardly. A big red blotch stained his left pants leg. One of the other riders led a horse with a man draped over the saddle. Soon two other riders came in with three more bodies across saddles.

The townspeople were shaking their heads. A doctor came out and began treating the wounded man in the street. Lassiter could see that Mitchell was seething with anger. If word got out that this town was too dangerous to travel to, there would be difficulty in getting Glitter Creek to prosper like it should. Right now this gang of road agents had Glitter Creek by the throat.

Harold Mitchell turned to Lassiter. His voice was a controlled growl. "You see what you're up against?"

Lassiter nodded. "Things will change," he said. "It might take a little time, but things around here will change."

3

BIG JACK SLOAN PACED the floor of the cabin while the remainder of his outlaw gang sat in silence. He was big and his dark features seemed even darker in anger. His hair was black and unkempt under his hat, and he had a heavy crop of eyebrows that pushed down over his already too small eyes, nearly hiding them.

The rest of the gang just looked at the floor. They had been listening to him yell for the last hour, and this was the first few seconds in all that time that he had been silent. It was hard to tell what he was thinking. You never knew what he was going to decide until he decided it. And sometimes it was crazy.

Sloan couldn't get over what had just happened to his plan to take over Glitter Creek. The plan had been simple: Harold Mitchell's daughter, Lanna, was on her way into Glitter Creek on the stage. They had known that for sure, since their contact in the bank had correctly gotten word to them.

He was a small and primpy man named Gil Driscoll,

who owned the only bank in town. Sloan would ride to one of the passes overlooking the valley and wait for Driscoll, who would ride up from Glitter Creek and convey important news.

Driscoll was shrewd and knew how to get things done without drawing attention. Sloan had never had any problems in meeting with Driscoll along the trail right on schedule. This deal with Harold Mitchell's daughter had been no exception. Driscoll had held up his end and brought the news accurately, right down to when the stage was supposed to arrive in Glitter Creek. But somehow things had gone wrong in getting Lanna Mitchell from the stage, and Sloan was looking for someone to blame it on.

Sloan had put four good men under his right-hand man—a slim outlaw with a dirty-blond beard and mustache and a knife scar under one eye. His name was Macey, and Sloan had known him since the gang had first formed. For a long time he and Macey had been real close; they had laughed and cried together and had robbed a lot of banks and stages together. Things had been real good then.

But it seemed as if Macey had suddenly gotten a wild streak in him, like he had learned all there was to learn about being a road agent and now he wanted his own gang. Sloan didn't want to have to kill Macey— he still cared some about the man, and besides, he was good with a gun.

So Sloan had figured a way to keep Macey's loyalty. He had told Macey there was a good amount of gold buried somewhere along the Mullen Road, and that some day, when they got too old to rob banks and stages, they would share it. He knew Macey would want in on the gold.

What he hadn't told Macey and never would was that there was no gold buried anywhere along the Mullen Road, at least none that he knew of. But it was a good way to keep Macey around and gunning for him, for the time being, anyway.

Sloan had given Macey four men and had told him to take care of the stage and bring Lanna Mitchell back to the hideout. Harold Mitchell would want his daughter back, and Glitter Creek would be theirs. Macey and the others had ridden up to wait for the stage. Easy pickings. It had all been set up so well. Then one man had stopped everything cold.

Some stranger dressed in black is what Macey had reported. Macey had been the only one to survive. That bothered Sloan a lot. Up to now Macey had never been one to back down from a fight. In fact, he relished it. This stranger in black must have been hell with a gun to drive Macey off like a rabbit.

Big Jack Sloan wondered to himself if maybe it wouldn't have happened if he had planned things differently. But Sloan didn't want to blame himself for what had occurred. He had had a feeling all along that he should have led the men to get Lanna Mitchell and let Macey take the remaining six over into the Selway to rob miners. As it had turned out, their luck at robbing hard-bitten miners had been considerably better than just knocking out a stagecoach.

"I can't understand what the hell happened up there," Sloan started in again. He was directing his questions to Macey. "One man comes along and five of you can't even stop him."

Macey had his arms folded in front of him. The scar under his eye was deepened with the lines in his face as his jaw muscles hardened in anger.

"I told you, Jack, we didn't figure to see him coming. He was just there all of a sudden and he opened fire. He wasn't one to miss, either."

Sloan wasn't about to give in to excuses. "I just wonder what happened is all. This stranger shoots Bill and Milt and Frank, and you turn tail like a rabbit. Then he gets Marty. Plus, he gets Mitchell's daughter back. And after all that, you can't find where he went with the girl. What am I supposed to think? Now we've got to start over—from scratch."

Sloan paced some more and looked out the doorway into the distance. Over the top of the mountain was the Mullen Road, where they had had considerable success in looting travelers over the last couple of years. Then they plan a method by which they can take full control of Glitter Creek and gain the profits from its growth, and some lone stranger comes along at just the right time and fouls it all up. One man. How could that be possible?

"Who in the hell was this stranger, anyway?" Sloan asked Macey. "And why did you let him shoot Marty?"

Macey looked down at the floor of the cabin and remained silent while all the others watched him. They all realized what disturbed Sloan the most was the fact that Marty had been killed. Marty, the youngest, had been a favorite of his. He had been bringing Marty along, teaching him things about planning robberies and how to get the drop on people. Marty had been wounded through the middle by the stranger and had died slowly. He would have been seventeen tomorrow.

Macey wanted to yell at Sloan. He wanted to ask him how he thought he should know who in hell the stranger was. He was just some rider dressed in black who had happened along. There wasn't any way to foresee that.

Macey had considered it and he decided now that he certainly wasn't going to tell Sloan how they had seen this stranger in black earlier. They had seen him at the trail crossing, where the sign to Glitter Creek pointed down the mountain. At that time they had considered taking him. But he was just one man and it would eat into their time. They needed to get to the stage. They hadn't figured this one man could stop them from doing what they wanted.

"One man don't do all that to me and get away with it," Sloan said. "You hear me, Macey? He ain't about to get away with killing Marty like that."

Macey slammed a boot into the floor, and his face came up toward Sloan. He decided no matter what Sloan thought, he would speak up then.

"What about the other three?" Macey asked. "Weren't they good men? They were all good men, and you got no right to wail about Marty like that."

There was silence in the room, and Sloan glared down at Macey. He couldn't very well tell Macey he was wrong, not in front of the others. He didn't want anyone to think he didn't care that the others were dead. He really didn't; they could be replaced. He just cared about Marty.

Sloan had realized all along that his relationship with Marty was causing trouble. It had gotten so that most of the men were wondering about Marty and why he was handed so many favors. It had gotten past the point that Marty had just been a kid and needed nurturing. It had gone beyond that.

Now Sloan was bitter about the kid's death, and he wasn't hiding it very well. He realized he had better get himself in order or the men would still turn against him. It would be better, Sloan decided, to drop the issue about Marty. Nothing was going to bring the kid back.

But there was still no reason why one man should have taken on five and come out on top. That he could hold over Macey and get away with.

"I'm worried about you, Macey," Sloan said. "You're put in charge of four men, and you let one man kill every one of them."

Macey ground his teeth together, and the muscles under his thin beard lumped up.

"Jack, I want you off my back over this. I told you we got chewed up by some stranger. I can't tell you no more. You'd best look him up yourself if you want to know more about him."

"Don't give me that, Macey," Sloan growled. "I put you in charge of men, I expect you to lead them, not run away and let them die."

Macey seethed for a moment. It wouldn't do any good to jump in the middle of Big Jack Sloan, even if he thought he could whip him. It was better to let Sloan put himself in bad with the others.

"Why didn't you have Marty with you?" Macey asked Sloan. "He's the one who caused the rest of them to get shot. He panicked."

Now the rest of the men looked to Sloan. Macey watched Sloan boil with anger. There was no way Sloan could prove him wrong. Macey was the only one who had survived. He could say what he wanted.

"Jack, you can't fret all day about this," Macey then said. "Marty's dead and the rest of them are dead. That's that."

"That isn't all there is to it," Sloan argued. "We

had Harold Mitchell's daughter right in our laps. We had Glitter Creek. Now it's all gone."

"If you want that woman so bad, I say we just ride down into town and take her," Macey said. "I told you that before. Now why don't we just do it?"

"Macey, do you want more men dead?" Sloan said sharply. "We ride into town, and we've got to ride back out again. We could get shot up doing that. We can't afford to lose any more men. Understand?"

"Who's to say we'd lose any more?"

"And why wouldn't we?" Sloan asked.

"They wouldn't figure us to do it," Macey argued. "They wouldn't figure us to be going in strong right away like that."

"It don't matter to me what you think," Sloan said. "We can't take the chance, not now."

"You're just broke up over Marty is all," Macey said.

"Don't push me, Macey," Sloan warned.

Macey watched Sloan pace the floor. All eyes were on Macey now, and he turned his face away from everyone. He remained quiet. He had argued with Sloan any number of times over how they were going to gain control of Glitter Creek. Sloan had wanted to do it right away, and Macey had argued that they let the town prosper a little, then move in slowly. With the banker on their side, they could easily suck money out of the economy without anybody really realizing it until it was too late.

But Big Jack Sloan was from the old school, where you rode in with power and might and you took control of things by blowing away anybody who stood in your path. Take it all right away and then control it. To Macey's way of thinking, it would be smarter to just let the town build and take things under control by sliding in gradually. Why shoot the place up? Let the banker do his work in a slick fashion. That way there was more money to be made for everybody, and for a lot longer period of time.

Now, during this argument and the bitterness over Marty's death, Macey had thought he could appease Sloan by taking his side for once and suggesting they ride in and take things under control right away. But Sloan had put him down again. It was obvious to Macey that Sloan was not really against his ideas so much; he was just against him. As far as Macey was concerned, things were going to have to change.

Finally Sloan quit pacing and walked out the door. He viewed the bodies of the four men who had been killed. They were lying just off to one side of the doorway all in a row. They weren't covered; Sloan wanted it that way. He wanted them to lie there with their lifeless eyes to the sky, looking up at the deep blue as they often had from their bedrolls in life. He figured they would want a last look into the sky before someone covered them with dirt.

He lingered near the body of the youngest, Marty, and a deep sadness came into his eyes. He wanted to kneel down and awaken him, but he knew better than to think any life would return. Already he was stiff in death and his skin was dark.

Sloan would be a long time in getting over Marty's death. Marty had been the son he had never had, the boy he had always wanted to follow in his footsteps when he was no longer able to lead the gang. There had been many nights in the past when Sloan had told Marty he would someday take the gang on outings to rob and loot. He had envisioned Marty leading the men, with them following like soldiers into battle. Maybe it was the battle part of it that affected Sloan most.

It wasn't that long ago that he had followed a Confederate commander, much like Marty had followed him. The commander's name was Cain, Colonel Anthony Cain. The colonel had nurtured him along much the same as he had nurtured Marty. The colonel had had great plans for him. Then Sloan had been right behind the colonel at Gettysburg when a Union bullet had taken Colonel Anthony Cain's life and left Sloan all alone in the world.

After standing over Marty for a considerable time, Sloan moved past the other two and stopped to look down at the one named Milt. He had been crippled, with one leg shorter than the other. Milt had just won a good horse from Sloan in a poker game—a sorrel stallion—and since it was gone when they had gone down to get the bodies, Sloan figured the stranger had taken it.

Sloan also figured this stranger dressed in black would likely keep that sorrel, as good as it was. Sloan would be looking for that stranger on that horse. Somehow he was going to have to kill that stranger.

Sloan didn't want to think about it, but the thought of the stranger reached deep into him and brought out a fear that no other man ever had. This stranger had to be good—and he had to have some kind of courage to stand up to five men and get all but one like he had. No man that could do that would be easy to kill. He would be impossible to face. Killing this stranger in black would take a lot of careful planning.

After looking at Marty one last time, Sloan went back into the cabin and told Macey to get a shovel.

"You have some men to bury," Sloan said.

"What? I ain't doing it alone."

Sloan stared hard at Macey. There was a sudden, hard look in Macey's eye that said he had been pushed too far. Sloan decided it wouldn't be wise to press Macey now, not after all that had happened and the pressure he was already under. It would be better to handle Macey another time.

"The rest of you draw cards to see which three draw burial duty with Macey," Sloan finally said. "But get it done. It's going to get dark before long."

Sloan couldn't make himself be on the hill where the men were digging Marty's grave. He didn't mind watching them bury the others, but he hated to face the reality that Marty was up there just as dead as the others and that he would never see the kid again.

When the grave for Marty was finished, Sloan hurried up the hill and told his men to back away and not to let Marty down into the grave just yet. He told them to go finish burying the others and to leave him alone with the kid.

When the others were gone, Sloan knelt down next to Marty's body. He peered into the young face. The body was starting to swell, but Sloan seemed to overlook that, as if Marty was just sleeping and that was all. Sloan was trying to make himself think Marty would open his eyes and come back to the cabin off the ground, just as soon as he asked him to.

"We've got work to do, kid," Sloan said to the body. "You can't be resting here all the time. We've got to get going so we can have that town for our own."

The more he talked to the dead kid the more Sloan realized he was making a fool of himself in front of the other men, who were gathered at the bottom of the hill talking. But Sloan didn't care what they thought. None of them could ever mean as much to him as Marty had; none of them were even close to Marty's worth.

Finally, Sloan covered Marty up in a blanket he had been wrapped in and eased him into the grave. Though Sloan felt the pain, he couldn't make himself cry. He couldn't remember the last time he had cried and he couldn't release the tightness in his chest. Marty was gone, and that was all there was to it now.

Sloan walked down the hill and told the men to go back up and fill in the graves. Sloan watched for a time, then turned toward the cabin. As he walked, a strange seething anger began working its way into Sloan. The more he thought about Lassiter, the more the anger would build itself. There wasn't anything more important to him now than getting that stranger dressed in black—that stranger they called Lassiter.

4

"THE SMELL OF OVERTURNED EARTH has always bothered me," Lassiter declared. "You people have buried a lot of men here. It's hard to smell the sage anymore."

It was late evening and there were a number of men gathered in the Glitter Creek Saloon for a meeting. With the recent developments along the Mullen Road in mind, Harold Mitchell had suggested they organize a town council and form a committee of men to govern the town and promote its development.

This first meeting was occurring three days after the holdup. It involved what action should be taken, if any, against the Sloan Gang, and how they should defend themselves against further attack. They were all listening to Lassiter, wondering who this stranger was that talked as if death were as close as his fingertips.

That afternoon they had buried the men who had gone out to find Lanna. Their graves were still piled with brown earth, and the town was still in depression.

Lassiter was working to get spirits raised again so that Glitter Creek could look forward and not into the past.

"You all have to understand that you're only as strong as your weakest link," Lassiter went on. "If you're going to stand up against someone as a group, make sure you pick men who will die for a cause. If you don't, one will let down. When that happens the rest will get uneasy and it's finished."

They all knew that Lassiter was working for Harold Mitchell and that Big Jack Sloan's gang had suffered the loss of at least three and maybe four men to Lassiter's guns. Lanna had told her father everything about the shootout, and he in turn had spread the word that at last a man had arrived who could stand against Sloan and his gang of killers.

Stand up against them was an understatement, Mitchell had told the townspeople. Lassiter had Sloan wondering if he would even be able to continue his thieving ways along the Mullen Road.

But Lassiter was used to people bragging him up— especially desperate people who suddenly saw a ray of hope emerging with his arrival. Lassiter knew it was going to be hard for Glitter Creek.

"As time goes by, things will get rougher here," Lassiter was saying. "That Sloan fellow will want this town worse now than he ever did. He will do crazy things to get it. Don't any of you be out of reach of a rifle."

"Where are you going to be at?" one man spoke up.

"I can't be here all the time," Lassiter answered. "I'm the shotgun rider on the stage, and people have to get in and out of here. Just remember what I told you about being armed. Once this is all over, you can all look ahead to prosperity."

Now they were looking to Harold Mitchell, who was standing off to one side of Lassiter. He had been watching and listening to Lassiter the whole time, and for once he had considerable confidence that Glitter Creek would remain alive and, as Lassiter had just said, could someday be prosperous. But it was going to take courage and hard work.

"I believe Mr. Lassiter has said about all that needs to be said," Mitchell commented. "Confidence in ourselves is the big factor here. We've lost some of our young men, our townspeople, and that hurts us. But we'll survive and we'll win. Just remember that— we'll win."

All the while Lassiter had paid close attention to one man among the crowd who exhibited concern rather than enthusiasm at having organized. Gil Driscoll, the banker, was standing by himself in one corner of the room. He was a small man with sharp features who seemed always to be tugging at his suit coat or some item of his clothes. He wore a thin gray tie that he pulled at frequently, giving the impression he was apt to strangle himself if he didn't stop.

Not once during the entire meeting did Driscoll ever look Lassiter in the eye. The other men were all alert and attentive and most of them asked questions. It made Lassiter wonder why one of the town's most visible and influential people was so downcast about a move that should have made him beam with delight.

"If we all support one another in this town," Mitchell was concluding, "we can't help but make this community grow and prosper. And with Mr. Lassiter here to help us with the road agent problem, we're on our way forward.''

The road agent problem was foremost on everyone's mind. It would fester there, Lassiter knew, until something was done about it. But that couldn't happen overnight; Sloan and his gang had built themselves up over time, and it would take time and planning to bring them down.

There were those who wanted to get a posse together and roust the Sloan Gang right away. They wanted their problems solved in short order so that their lives could get into a normal flow and their worries would be less involved with merely staying alive. Many of them were willing to risk their lives initially in a posse to hopefully remove later worry.

But in listening to Lassiter, they all realized it was best to gather forces and wait for the outlaws to come to them. Men who had gone out before had come back across a saddle. That could easily happen again, and with no guarantee that the Sloan Gang would be finished. Better to stay in town where they knew the territory. Up in the hills the outlaws had the advantage; here in Glitter Creek the townspeople had the edge.

The edge is what was important in this whole thing, Lassiter knew. There was no doubt Big Jack Sloan knew what an edge could do, and as it happened in so many places he had been before, Lassiter knew Glitter Creek had to have someone who sided with Sloan and wanted the town in his hands.

Lassiter realized now was not the time to suggest to the men at the meeting that they should be watching for someone among them. That could easily do more harm than good and create disharmony as each man looked to the other with mistrust. And if he told them to all keep an eye on Gil Driscoll, that would make Driscoll ever more cautious and likely drive him to cause money problems with the town. If Driscoll was working for Sloan, sooner or later everyone would know.

"I suggest all those interested meet here again next Wednesday evening," Harold Mitchell said. "We have a lot of ground to cover."

The meeting broke up and the men left with renewed vigor. Lassiter stood in the doorway of the saloon and watched the men go to their horses and return home. Lassiter was watching Gil Driscoll in particular. He was crossing the street in the direction of the Glitter Creek Bank.

"That's Gil Driscoll, the president of the bank," Harold Mitchell told Lassiter. "I should have introduced you to him."

"Maybe you can do that soon," Lassiter said. "He's a man I would like to talk to for a little while."

"I think you and he would get along fine," Mitchell said. "Everyone in town likes him."

"I presume he has a lot of influence around town," Lassiter said.

"Yes, he does. I sense that he bothers you in some way. Am I right?"

"I watched him during the meeting, and I can't say that he seemed happy with how things went," Lassiter answered. "I guess it seems to me that he should have asked a few questions and raised an eyebrow now and then. He just stood there looking at the floor."

"He's a quiet man, Lassiter," Mitchell spoke up. "I don't want to sound like I'm defending him. I think he should have participated more in the discussion.

But that's just the way he is. He's a good friend of mine and I know him well. He runs a good bank."

Lassiter nodded. "Well, I came in here cold to who's friends with who. I can see things objectively from the outside. And I think your friend Driscoll bears watching."

Harold Mitchell was taken aback at Lassiter's frank opinion. Finally he shrugged. "You are entitled to your own opinion. But I don't know why you feel that way about Gil Driscoll."

"It's just a feeling I have," Lassiter said. "How long have you known him?"

Mitchell thought a moment. "About three years, I'd say. He came about a year after Glitter Creek got a post office. He loaned me the money to get my hotel and mining interests started. I owe that man a great deal."

"Was it his money he loaned you?" Lassiter asked.

"Well, I really don't know. I assume so, but I never asked. I don't know why I should have asked, do you, Mr. Lassiter?"

Lassiter was silent for a moment, leaning against the door frame. His eyes were still on the bank.

"A man who comes into town and loans out money is a man who is looking to own the town," Lassiter said. "Even if you pay the debt back to him in full, you still owe him."

Harold Mitchell took a deep breath. Lassiter could tell he was getting aggravated. Gil Driscoll was one subject that had never come up in a discussion of this kind before. It was making Mitchell wonder why Lassiter would question the integrity of someone who was considered a pillar of the community.

"I don't owe Gil Driscoll in that sense," Mitchell

said defensively. "He has never made any demands on me. None whatsoever."

"Do you spend a lot of time with him?"

"Quite a bit. We play poker together with some of the other businessmen in town. In fact, we have a game scheduled upstairs tonight."

"I see him here quite a bit," Lassiter said. "He eats here regularly. He must not be married."

"No," Mitchell said, "he doesn't have a wife. He lives alone. There is a woman here he knows, however. She is alone herself and is starting a dry goods store. I'm sure you understand."

"I'm just concerned about his future plans for the town," Lassiter said. "His personal life is his own."

"So what besides his shy personality causes you concern?" Mitchell wanted to know.

"Are you sure he's as shy as he puts on?"

"I know him very well," Mitchell said.

"How much do you tell him about your affairs?"

Mitchell cleared his throat. "Mr. Lassiter, I am enough of a professional to know where to draw the line with information. I think I am a capable judge of character."

"I'm not saying you aren't. I'm saying that you can become friends with someone and that person can change, but you won't see it too readily. You won't want to think it's happening. Did you tell Driscoll about Lanna coming to town from San Francisco?"

"A lot of people knew about that," Mitchell answered. "That was no secret. I was delighted that she was coming. Gil Driscoll was happy for me."

Lassiter nodded. He continued to watch the bank.

He could see Driscoll looking out one of the windows toward the saloon.

"I have to say that I think you're wrong about Gil Driscoll," Mitchell told Lassiter. "He's been a friend and a staunch supporter of this town ever since he came here. I can't see that he wouldn't want anything but the best for this community."

"I hope you're right," Lassiter said. He turned from the doorway and walked over to the bar. After quickly downing a whiskey he ordered another and stood sipping on it. Mitchell watched from the doorway for a time, then came over and joined him.

"When do you think we should start up the stage lines again?" he asked Lassiter. "There are people wondering when the mail is going to come in."

"I'm ready," Lassiter answered. "Do you have a full load?"

"I believe we do. I know there are a lot of passengers who have been wondering about the run along points west of here. Besides just mail service, there are a lot of people who want to come to this town. We just have to get them here."

"We'll get them here," Lassiter said, downing the second whiskey. "But they had all better be used to gunplay. Sloan will want blood. It will be hard getting through the first time around, especially after I shot up his bunch as bad as I did. He'll be waiting for me."

"You don't seem afraid," Mitchell observed.

"It pays to be cautious," Lassiter commented, "not afraid."

"I understand," Mitchell said. "We'll schedule a run for the end of the week. Will that work?"

"It should," Lassiter said with a nod. "Maybe we ought to take some men up onto the ridge the first time out, just to discourage Sloan. I'd bet he will be there waiting, but he won't come at us if there are a lot of men with rifles waiting for him."

Mitchell smiled broadly. "That is a very good idea," he said. "That way Sloan won't know what to expect on subsequent runs."

"That's the idea," Lassiter said with a nod. "Keep him guessing."

Mitchell excused himself to join the others in the businessmen's poker game upstairs. He began the climb upstairs, thinking about the man he had hired as shotgun rider for his stage lines. He couldn't remember ever meeting a man quite like this gunfighter dressed in black.

Mitchell realized there wasn't anyone who could guess what Lassiter was thinking. And he couldn't get over Lassiter's cool confidence. Here was a man who didn't appear afraid of anyone or anything—yet he wasn't brazen about how he held the upper hand. Lassiter was a man who knew the odds and how to play them.

The more Harold Mitchell thought about it, the more he could understand why people who wished to cause trouble feared Lassiter. He wore twin Colts that rested one on each hip, their black handles polished from use. His cartridge belts crossed and were jammed with bullets. They fit his waist as if they had been molded to it.

On the other hand, he didn't seem to intimidate people with whom he shared conversation on a general basis. Women especially seemed attracted to him. They didn't seem to fear him, but held him in awe. After what he had accomplished to save Lanna, he was the talk of the town.

Harold Mitchell was also noticing that Lanna was watching Lassiter more and more as the days passed. He wanted to think it was just a sort of infatuation that had come with Lassiter's saving her from being kidnapped by the Sloan Gang. That was understandable; but Harold Mitchell was hoping it wouldn't last.

Mitchell was hoping that sooner or later Lanna would strike up a relationship with Gil Driscoll. That would make things run very smooth in town. But he hadn't realized how Lanna had become such a woman of her own thinking. Being with her mother in the city had made his daughter think for herself. It didn't look as if she was going to become excited about Gil Driscoll.

None of that really mattered until the Sloan Gang was finished. What was important now was getting the stage lines back in operation and making Glitter Creek a safe and properous place to live.

As Harold Mitchell topped the stairs he turned and looked back down at Lassiter, still drinking at the bar. His own confidence rose another rung. This man—this Lassiter who had ridden in dressed in black—was more than a match for Big Jack Sloan and his gang. He was going to take them out to the last man—just so Sloan didn't have any ideas Lassiter hadn't already thought of himself.

At the bar Lassiter could feel Mitchell's eyes on him. It wasn't as if people didn't stare at him all the time; they did, and they wondered all the time what he was made of. But Mitchell was not just curious, Lassiter knew. Mitchell was also concerned that everything was going to work out as nice as pie and that everybody he liked was going to be good and everybody he didn't like was going to turn out to be bad.

Lassiter knew that was going to be a problem. Harold Mitchell was bound to be disappointed when it was all over. And it was going to be Gil Driscoll who caused all the disappointment.

5

IN THE PAST GIL DRISCOLL had found it easy to ride up from Glitter Creek for his weekly meetings with Big Jack Sloan. Since he lived alone, he was seldom missed after banking hours, and it was widely known that he occasionally traveled on horseback to the nearby settlements to see how they were prospering. It was certainly in the back of everyone's mind that establishing banking systems in towns was a priority for a banker.

But now things were beginning to be different. The reason was the stranger named Lassiter. Driscoll had found him particularly nosy and disturbing. During the town meeting in the saloon after the stage holdup, Driscoll had noticed Lassiter watching him intently. This had bothered Driscoll to the point that he wondered if this stranger in black could read minds.

There was still the matter of keeping in contact with Big Jack Sloan, stranger or not. Driscoll had been working too long and too hard toward the day when he could sit in the bank and control the purse strings of everyone in the entire town. He wanted to be able to make the decisions on money and development. Big Jack Sloan had promised him that—if he would just cooperate in getting the town under Sloan's control.

Driscoll realized now that it was going to be harder and harder to make contact with Lassiter around. The stranger had taken to watching him carefully and had even tried to get Harold Mitchell to see that something was wrong at the bank. This had infuriated Driscoll. But there wasn't a thing he could do about it.

Now, as he rode through the late evening up toward the pass where he always met Sloan, he thought of seeing Lassiter's body draped over a horse. That would solve a lot of problems. With the next raid on the stage, that was a possibility. He would make that point to Sloan.

Sloan was already at the pass waiting for him when he got there. The big man was sitting his horse easily, watching out along the trail that led below onto the Mullen Road. This trail through the pass took off from the road, and anyone coming up here could be spotted from over a mile away.

"You're late getting up here," Sloan told Driscoll.

"That stranger, Lassiter, he's been watching me," Driscoll explained. "He's trouble."

"Listen, we buried four men because of him," Sloan said. "I'm a little irritated, to say the least. The next person that goes into the ground is this Lassiter. That's his name—Lassiter?"

"That's what Harold Mitchell and his daughter call him," Driscoll said with a nod.

"Is he still riding that big sorrel he took when he shot up my men?"

Driscoll nodded. "He seems to like that horse a lot."

"The son of a bitch," Sloan snarled. "I want that horse and his hide, both. Lassiter, you say his name is. . . ."

Driscoll nodded again. "What are you thinking about?"

"Why does that name strike me?" Sloan wondered out loud. He thought a moment. "It doesn't matter," he finally said. "When is the stage running again?"

"This weekend," Driscoll answered. "But I wouldn't plan on stopping it if I were you."

"Why not?"

"Because there's going to be a posse with it."

Sloan cursed loudly and slammed his fist into the pommel of his saddle.

"I want that Lassiter dead. I want him dead right away. I don't want to wait on it. The men are antsy enough about him. I want to kill him."

Driscoll listened to Sloan rave. It didn't do any good to try and stop him. He always had to get it out of his system before you could say anything else to him that he even listened to. Sloan was that kind of man.

But Driscoll didn't find that particularly awkward. He knew that once Sloan was finished spouting off, he would be ready to listen. And that was when Driscoll usually got to say what he wanted and how he wanted things done.

That was what made Driscoll so happy about his relationship with Big Jack Sloan. All the while Sloan thought he had control. He was big and forceful and when he talked, people were quiet. They didn't always listen, but they were quiet.

Then when he was quiet, it was as if he were in a

blank stage of some kind—like his mind was empty. Driscoll had learned how to use that to his advantage. He would let Sloan finish, and then he would start telling Sloan the best way to handle situations. Driscoll would always make it sound like Sloan was coming up with the ideas, and then Sloan would nod and say that was what they should do.

It was in the back of Gil Driscoll's mind to some-day control both Glitter Creek and the Sloan Gang. That would have been easy enough if Lassiter hadn't stepped in.

If that hadn't happened it would all be over right now. Lanna Mitchell would be at the hideout, and Harold Mitchell would be willing to give the town up to get her back. Some other men might not do that, but Harold Mitchell would.

Driscoll was thinking how easy it would have been to just agree with Mitchell and gather up all the money they could find and then sign deeds to property and mining interests and everything else over to Big Jack Sloan. Then it would be all over, and Glitter Creek would have actually been his.

"How did you learn about the posse?" Sloan asked Driscoll.

"We had a poker game the other night," Driscoll answered. "After the game Mitchell and I had some whiskey and Mitchell's tongue started wagging, like it always does when he drinks. I can learn a lot from him that way."

"Well, I want to see Lassiter killed," Sloan said. "How do you suppose I can do that?"

"We're going to have to figure things more carefully now," Driscoll said to Sloan. "I know that once the stage gets up on the ridge and only Lassiter is guarding it, then you can lead your men against him and finish it. But you're going to have to let me tell you when that is. Don't get impatient. It will happen.''

"So what do we do in the meantime?" Sloan wanted to know.

"I would suggest you go and find yourself some more men to fill in for the four Lassiter killed," Driscoll suggested. "You're going to have to be at full strength if you want to take Glitter Creek when the time is right."

"Yeah, you're right," Sloan said with a nod. "We'd best go and find some more men."

"You might try Bannack, across the pass into Montana Territory," Driscoll suggested. "They had a sheriff named Plummer who led a gang some time back. But they hanged him. Now I heard they've got some more men in jail over there awaiting a town trial. If you went over and broke them out, I'd wager they would be grateful enough to join your gang."

Sloan smiled broadly. "Maybe that wouldn't be such a bad idea. Them kind of boys would fit in pretty good. And if they figured to get paid some real money, they would want to ride with us for sure."

Driscoll nodded. "As soon as you get more men and there's a stage run without a posse, I'll let you know and you can get rid of Lassiter."

"Damn right!" Sloan said with a nod.

Driscoll watched Sloan ride back over the pass toward the hideout, thinking to himself that he was getting more control over Sloan each time they met. Now Sloan would go back and he and his men would ride over the mountains into Bannack and they would add men to the depleted ranks of their gang. And Driscoll would go back to Glitter Creek and learn more about what was going to happen there—and hopefully how they could get rid of the dangerous stranger named Lassiter.

Dawn broke over the crags of the mountains and found Lassiter riding the big roan to the top of a small pass above the Mullen Road. There had been a thundershower earlier in the night, and the air was fresh and clean. But Lassiter knew this wasn't going to be a ride during which he could enjoy the beauty of the land around him.

He was a distance from Glitter Creek, and he knew this was a place well traveled by other than honorable people. He was up off the Mullen Road, headed for the place the townsfolk referred to as Miner Canyon. It was wild and desolate and likely housed road agents.

Late the afternoon before, Lassiter had watched Driscoll ride into town from somewhere in this direction. Driscoll had then come into the saloon and had been so pleased with himself that for the first time he had looked into Lassiter's eyes. That had convinced Lassiter that without a doubt, Driscoll was tied in with the Sloan Gang.

Having Driscoll look at him directly had pleased Lassiter. It had showed that Driscoll had gained a lot of confidence and at the same time a lot of foolish pride. Lassiter had stared back hard and Driscoll's glare had melted down like butter.

Driscoll would never look him straight on like that again, Lassiter knew. But that one time had been enough to convince Lassiter beyond a doubt that he should be trailing Driscoll whenever he could.

This trail he was on now, far back in the pines, had to lead to someplace where many horsemen traveled often. The trail was worn down by shod hooves and the imprints showed where riders had gone in both directions—too far off the main trail to be used by ordinary travelers.

Lassiter could see a great distance in all directions from here. Now that the sun was rising, the mountains were a deep blue, and cottony clouds drifted along the timberline. Overhead, eagles glided in large circles above the immense expanse of rolling timber and broad valley below.

Lassiter checked his rifle and his pistols to be sure they were loaded fully. He had decided he was going to ride this trail up over the pass and see where it took him. If his notion was right, it could lead him to Big Jack Sloan and his gang of road agents.

Determined not to ride into an ambush of some sort, Lassiter took his time. He rode the big sorrel along the trail through the dense stands of pine and, higher up, fir and spruce. Never once did the trail leave the cover. It wound its way through the trees for a good long ways and finally came out in a little secluded valley surrounded by trees and rocks.

Lassiter waited for a time, looking and listening. He could hear birds singing their summer songs in the trees, and he could see where a little stream broke from the slopes just a ways down below. And as he looked harder, he thought he could see a cabin hidden back among a dense stand of quaking aspen.

It would be foolish to ride in down there, Lassiter figured, so he tied the sorrel to a tree and took his rifle from the saddle scabbard. Moving cautiously, he made his way down the hill toward the stand of aspens.

Taking a stand in the aspens, Lassiter watched the cabin for a while. He could see no one about and he could hear no one inside. Just in front of the cabin was a large corral, where three horses were standing, switching their tails against the flies. Nothing else stirred.

Lassiter walked down to the cabin. Hanging from a big tree near the door was a side of elk. Hanging next to it were just the hind quarters of a deer. Both animals had been hurriedly butchered and were covered with hides. Startled magpies flew from where they had been trying to poke their bills through the hides, scolding as they rose into the sky.

Lassiter went into the cabin and took his time looking around inside. It appeared as if a number of men lived here, but were now gone for some reason. The inside showed it had been occupied as early as the night before and whoever was living there certainly intended to come back.

There were any number of bedrolls scattered around on small bunks and on the dirt floor over cuts of fir bough and leaves. Extra pants and shirts lay strewn or in piles in the corners and along the walls.

In addition there were two blackened coffeepots atop a cookstove, and scraps of bread, meat, and beans littered the tops of two tables. A squirrel ran past Lassiter out the door with a crust of bread in its mouth.

Lassiter knew he had found the outlaw stronghold. Big Jack Sloan and his gang of road agents lived here. But where were they now?

That was a question he knew he couldn't answer. But he decided it wouldn't be wise to be caught inside if the gang suddenly decided to show up.

Lassiter went outside and studied the country around him. Sloan lived in a small and hidden little canyon just over the mountain from the ridge where the Mullen Road traveled. This must be what Harold Mitchell had referred to as Miner Canyon. But the main part of the canyon was farther down a ways, over a small spur of rocks and timber. This was a perfect place for a hideout.

Now that Lassiter realized where he was and how he could get out without using the same trail he had come in on, he decided he would take the first step in getting rid of Big Jack Sloan and his gang.

Lassiter went out to the corral and opened the gate. He let the horses out and made sure they were running over the spur of rocks and timber down into the main part of Miner Canyon. Then he went back inside the cabin and found some lanterns filled with kerosene.

The bedrolls went up in a burst when doused with the kerosene and touched with a flame, and soon the log walls were also ablaze. Lassiter hurried out and up to where his horse was tied. He climbed on the sorrel and took the trail the three horses had followed down into the main part of the canyon.

He looked back once just before he went out of sight into the timber. The cabin was now a large blotch of flames against the hillside. He didn't worry about setting the surrounding forest afire, as the grass and trees were still wet from the thundershower. It was just the cabin that burned, and Lassiter knew it would give Big Jack Sloan something to worry about.

6

IT WAS VERY LATE in Bannack, well past midnight, but the streets were still active. Music and laughter blared from the saloons, and the sounds of men crossing back and forth could be heard a long ways off.

As far as Macey was concerned, it wasn't the best night to be breaking men out of a jail. They didn't even know the town of Bannack—this being the first time they had ever seen it—and what was worse, they had no way of knowing how well the jail was guarded.

"Do you think we ought to try it?" Macey asked Sloan.

"Yes, we're going in there," Sloan said without hesitation. "We need men and that jail's got them. They'll be glad to ride with us."

"What's to say those men are still even in the jail?"

Sloan turned toward Macey and his voice was harsh in the darkness.

"Macey, if you're so yellow, you can stay up here and wait for us."

"No call to talk like that," Macey said. "I was just

56

thinking that we could be in trouble if we was to ride down there and find that jail empty."

"Driscoll told me there was men in that jail," Sloan insisted. "He was here. He ought to know. Now, the rest of us are ridin' down in there. You with us?"

"I'm with you," Macey finally said.

Macey had been trying to talk Sloan out of getting more men ever since he had come back down from the pass, where he had met with the banker, Driscoll. Though Sloan wouldn't tell Macey what had been discussed, Macey was sure that Sloan wasn't smart enough to understand what Driscoll was up to. Driscoll had his own ideas of what was going to happen, and he was manipulating Sloan pretty well up to now. Driscoll was putting all kinds of ideas into Sloan's head, and to Macey's way of thinking, it was jeopardizing his own takeover of the gang.

Macey realized that there was no argument that the gang needed more men. They had lost control of the Mullen Road now, and that stranger had the upper hand. But the men to be taken into the gang should be selected and not just taken from some dirty jail cell. Driscoll's recommendation was not at all favorable in Macey's opinion. Who knew these men? Would they be loyal or would they try and take the gang over for themselves? Maybe Driscoll had set things up against them.

Macey had been worrying about this ever since they had left the hideout to ride over the mountains and into the Montana Territory. It would be hard to come in here and just do what they wanted. Though it had been some years before, a real bad one named Henry Plummer had gotten himself hanged over here. These citizens had their own ways of dealing with road agents, and they weren't partial to gangs of men who broke thieves out of jail.

The other thing that was in the back of Macey's mind was the gold that Sloan had talked about when they had first met. Macey had brought it up any number of times over the past few months, and Sloan had just said, "When the time comes, Macey, when the time comes," at the end of each conversation. Now Macey was beginning to wonder if there even was any gold.

It was certain in Macey's mind that if there was any gold buried somewhere, he was going to have to get the information out of Sloan fairly soon. With more men coming into the gang, Macey was getting uneasy.

They got close to town and the music and noise grew louder. It sounded as if someone had made a big gold strike somewhere and was treating the town to a party. They stopped their horses in a small draw at the edge of town and watched through the moonlight.

"There's a lot of men in the streets," Macey told Sloan. "Maybe we hadn't ought to try this."

Sloan blew out his breath. "Listen, Macey, we didn't ride clean over them mountains for a picnic. We'll get them men Driscoll talked about out of the jail and we'll get out of here. Just get them out and leave. Simple as that."

Sloan was always considering things simple, and it angered Macey. Nothing was ever simple. Going into a town and a jail they knew nothing about and breaking men out wasn't going to be simple by any means.

"You want us to have Glitter Creek, don't you?" Sloan asked Macey.

"Sure," Macey said with a nod. "But I ain't sure this is the way we're going to get it done. This damn town is a long ways from our territory. They hang people here."

"I thought we just talked about this," Sloan said.

"We couldn't see anything from the hill," Macey said. "Now we get down here and the place is packed with people. We can't shoot them all should gunplay break out."

Macey knew he was right in this argument. He could tell the other men were getting nervous and beginning to side with him. Bannack's streets were loaded with drunken miners, and people like that might shoot at anything just for the fun of it.

"You scared?" Sloan asked.

"Just thinking, is all," Macey said. "I still wonder why you think so much of Driscoll. How do you really know for sure there are even any men over here? Maybe that banker wants you dead so he can have the town to himself."

Some of the men began to talk among themselves, and Sloan sat silent on his horse for a time, looking through the moonlight at Macey. He hadn't thought of that.

"I just don't know why you put so much trust in Driscoll is all," Macey said again.

"There ain't no reason for him to lie to me," Sloan defended Driscoll. "He knows he can't get that town without us. Especially since that Lassiter came. Driscoll knows it's got to be us who kills Lassiter."

Sloan had a point and Macey conceded. It was certain that this stranger named Lassiter would have to be killed or driven away if they were to take over the town. Since the stranger had already killed four of the gang, there was little sense in thinking he could be driven away. Their only hope was to kill him.

And to do that they would need all the manpower they could get. There was sense in thinking that once Lassiter was dead, the other problems would work themselves out.

"Well, maybe we need these men," Macey conceded. "I just hope Driscoll is right."

They looked down into the town for a time, determining where the jail was and the best way to get there without being noticed. It would work, they decided, if they rode around the edge of the town and descended upon the jail and got the men out as quickly as possible. Sloan and two of the gang would go into the jail while Macey and the others remained outside.

At the jail things seemed quiet—too quiet. Sloan got down from his horse and drew his pistol. There wasn't even a light on inside the jail.

"Great," Macey told Sloan. "That Driscoll just played you for a fool, and we're all in on it."

"Shut up!" Sloan hissed. He ordered two of the men with Macey to go up the street a ways and bring two horses apiece back with them. They might need them if they were going to break men out of jail.

"Just stay out here and wait, and tell us if somebody comes," Sloan then told Macey.

Sloan crept through the shadows toward the jail, with two of the gang behind him. He tried the door and found it locked. He cursed, then kicked and kicked at the door until it broke through.

"Forget it!" Macey said from his horse. "Hell, this is crazy!"

Sloan was inside the jail in the darkness. He heard rustling somewhere toward the back and then a voice.

"Who is it?"

Sloan and the others were quiet. The voice from the jail cell called out once again.

"I said who the hell is it?"

Sloan then stepped forward, his gun pointed in the darkness.

"Who's in that cell?"

"You ain't no jailkeeper," the voice spoke up. "What are you here for?"

One of Sloan's men found a lantern on a desk and a box of stick matches beside it. When the lantern was lit, Sloan took it and held it up.

There were two men sharing a single cell. The one who had been talking was standing with his hands on the bars, peering through. He was tall and thin and close to thirty, with dark hair and an odd smile on his face. He didn't seem particularly frightened, but he was very curious.

There was another, younger man standing behind him. He was light-complected and held no expression. The two continued to peer out, and the dark-featured man in front spoke again.

"Where did you men come from?"

"That doesn't matter," Sloan said. "Why are you in here without a jailer?"

"They're all celebrating some new strike over the hill," the dark-featured one answered. "If you're here to hang us, get it over with. But I didn't figure it would happen till morning."

"We got a trial coming," the younger man said quickly. "You can't do what you did to the others."

"The others?" Sloan said. "What happened to the others?"

"I guess they hung four men just two days past,"

the dark-featured one said. "They got caught stealin' horses."

Sloan cursed again. He had gotten here too late to add many men to his gang. The dark-featured one might work in all right, but he had his doubts about the younger one.

But then he remembered that Marty had started out the same way—reluctant and unsure of himself. This young man wasn't as big as Marty had been, but he was blond like Marty. With a little training he might work out at that.

"Why are you two in here?" Sloan asked.

"I took some gold from a miner," the dark-featured one said. "This one helped me. I still ain't figured why you're here."

"You want to ride with us?" Sloan asked them. "We'll get you out and you can join up with us."

"Who are you?" the dark-featured man asked.

"I told you, that don't matter right now," Sloan said. "We've got to get you out of here, if you plan to ride with us."

"Sure we'll ride with you," the dark-featured one said. "Get us out and we'll go anywhere with you."

He pointed to a drawer at one end of a desk and told them to look for the keys there. He said their guns were in the next drawer down.

The younger one protested. "I don't think I want to go. I ain't done nothing bad enough yet. I don't want to ride with road agents."

"Sure you do," Sloan said. "We make lots of money. You could get rich."

Suddenly Macey was inside. "What the hell are you doing? Someone's coming."

Sloan was unlocking the jail door, and he turned to

tell Macey to get the rest of the men ready to go. Then they heard yelling not far from the jail, and it was coming closer.

By the time they got outside, there were a number of men coming up the street. They were talking among themselves and pointing through the darkness. Sloan took a rifle from a scabbard on his saddle and opened fire.

Two of the approaching men fell immediately. The others scattered and there was a sudden hail of gunfire from along the edge of the street. One of the stolen horses fell.

Sloan ordered them all to ride out. Bullets came faster through the darkness now. The blond kid began to yell about not wanting to go, but suddenly a man appeared from behind a building with a gun and the kid shot him. It was an instinctive reaction, but the man fell dead.

"You haven't got much choice now," Sloan told him. He helped the kid onto one of the stolen horses, and they all turned toward the edge of town.

7

Sloan led Macey and the rest of the gang through the mountains out of Montana Territory and into Idaho Territory. Sloan had been quiet since leaving Bannack with just the two men they had broken out of jail. The older one's name was Coleman, and he mentioned he had fought for the Confederacy in the war. He talked a lot, saying all the time that he liked shooting and that he could do the gang a lot of good.

That Coleman had fought with the Confederacy was a plus as far as Sloan was concerned. No one was sure yet how good he was at shooting, though Coleman obviously thought of himself as a marksman of some sort. He talked about all the men he had shot and all the robberies he had been in on. No one knew how much was blown up, but he showed scars on his arms and on his chest and stomach to prove some of his stories were true.

Sloan appeared impressed with Coleman at times, but he was more interested in the younger man, whose name was Donny Jenks. Since killing the man on the street in Bannack, Jenks had been withdrawn and sullen. A typical mood for a young kid who has just killed his first man, Sloan thought. The kid would come out of it in time, and he would make a good member of the Sloan Gang. Maybe not as good as Marty had been, but nonetheless a good outlaw.

But as they rode, Macey could tell that Donny Jenks wasn't any more interested in becoming a part of the Sloan Gang than when he had been taken from the jail cell. He had killed a man, but that didn't mean he was obligated to kill more. Not one of the townspeople in Bannack had any idea that he had killed that man. It could have been any one of them.

The day passed into afternoon, and each man rode silently with his own thoughts. When they got to the edge of Miner Canyon, everyone noticed the little wisps of smoke coming from down in the canyon— from right where the cabin should be.

They got down to where the cabin had been and found nothing but charred logs. Smoke was still curling up from places in thin streams that lifted and dissipated into the air. Sloan got down from his horse and inspected the ruins, saying nothing. Macey and the others watched in silence. Sloan was so mad he had not even let it out by cursing. He was holding it in, and that wasn't a good sign.

Everyone wondered how the cabin had been burned. But it was plain that someone had set the fire, for the horses were gone as well. The gate was open and there was no sign that the horses had broken through anywhere. Whoever had set them free wasn't hiding anything. And that meant the stranger, Lassiter, had somehow found his way down into the canyon.

Everything in the cabin had been destroyed, including extra guns and ammunition and a lot of clothes and personal items. The only things left were what had been outside, including a few axes and some horse tack resting under a tarp behind some trees. There was nothing left to do but start over.

"Let's clear out this burned stuff and get to work on another cabin," Sloan finally said. Everyone sat their horses for a moment and finally Sloan blared, "Now! I said get a new cabin up now!"

Sloan's voice was louder than Macey had ever heard it before, and he took it upon himself to immediately direct some of the men to cutting logs while the others dragged burned timbers and other debris off the old foundation. When Macey had the men working, Sloan called him aside.

"You know as well as I do who did this, don't you?" Sloan said to Macey.

"I figure it was Lassiter," Macey said with a shrug.

"It had to be Lassiter," Sloan said. "But how did he find our hideout?"

Macey looked at Sloan for a time. "I think you know the answer to that one, if you'd think about it."

"You mean Driscoll?"

Macey nodded. "Of course. Likely Lassiter followed him up to where you and he meet. Don't that seem reasonable?"

Sloan thought about it for a moment. He was looking across the canyon where the trail wound up the steep slope into the timber.

"I can't see no other way," Sloan said. He was thinking about Driscoll, wondering how they were going to get together in the future now that Lassiter knew both the meeting place and the location of the hideout.

Macey could see that Sloan was getting ever more concerned about how he was going to take over Glitter Creek and get rid of Lassiter at the same time. Driscoll was making it harder and harder to do that. Somehow Lassiter must have gotten suspicious of Driscoll and followed his tracks at one time or another. Macey was eager now to drive his point home about how little he cared for Driscoll.

"I told you that banker was trouble. Now you can see that he doesn't pay any attention to what's going on. He just rode up here and didn't even know that Lassiter was trailing him. Now we're going to have more trouble."

"We're not going to have more trouble," Sloan said matter-of-factly. "Driscoll is going to tell us when the next stage run is, and then we're going to be there and that will be it. First Lassiter shoots up my men, and now he burns our cabin. The next stage run, we're going to be there."

"Won't Lassiter be looking for us?" Macey asked.

"I don't care," Sloan said. "I'm going to get that Lassiter if it's the last thing I ever do."

Lassiter sat in on the town council meeting, resting comfortably in his chair next to Harold Mitchell. During the meeting they had been discussing the future of the town and how they were in a position to do some real expansion. Another creek filled with gold had been discovered just over the hill, and everyone was coming from all over to mine it.

As a result, activity on the creeks close to town had improved, and Harold Mitchell had just opened a mine that led into a tunnel above one of the creeks. His men were bringing gold out already, and Mitchell was having Lassiter guard the workers when he wasn't riding shotgun on the stage.

Things were running more smoothly now that the Sloan Gang was temporarily out of business. Lassiter had reported his burning of their hideout cabin, to the cheers of all the businessmen present, but had warned that Sloan wouldn't be stopped that easily. He would just build another cabin and go right ahead from there.

Lassiter noticed Driscoll had said little during the entire meeting. He had been as surprised as the others at hearing the cabin had been burned. He had given a mock cheer to try and fit in with the other whoops and yells, but Lassiter had seen through it clearly.

Toward the end of the meeting Lassiter began to watch Driscoll so closely that it made him extremely nervous.

"Do you think Sloan and his men will try and rob your bank?" Lassiter asked him.

"It's your job to see that he doesn't," Driscoll promptly replied.

"If I'm guarding the stage or watching the mine, who's to say he and his men won't hit town and go straight for your bank?" Lassiter asked.

"Sloan and his men have never been down into town before," Driscoll said. "Never have they come into this town for anything. Why should they start now?"

"How do you know they haven't?" Lassiter asked. "Do you know Sloan or any of his men?"

"Of course not!" Driscoll answered quickly. "I resent your attitude, Mr. Lassiter. How could I possibly know any of those men?"

"You seemed confident in saying that none of them

had ever been into town," Lassiter answered. "I was just curious as to why you were so sure."

"I don't know why you dislike me so, Mr. Lassiter," Driscoll said. "But I won't stand for any more of this. Good evening, gentlemen."

Driscoll got up from the table and left everyone speechless as he took his coat and top hat from a coat rack and walked out of the bank into the street. Everyone turned their attention to Lassiter and Harold Mitchell, who was telling Lassiter he had spoken out of turn.

"I don't know why you insist on making life so miserable for that man," Mitchell was saying. "What has he done to make you so sure that he's somehow tied in with Sloan and his gang?"

Lassiter was aware that all the businessmen were listening intently. Some, Lassiter knew, sided with him against Driscoll. But others—most notably the main man in town, Harold Mitchell—seemed to think that Driscoll was getting undue criticism from Lassiter.

"How do you think I found that cabin that I burned?" Lassiter asked Mitchell. "The other day I followed where Driscoll's horse had left tracks going out of town. That day he hadn't gone to any towns nearby, like he always says he does. That day he went up into the mountains outside of town. The tracks took me to a pass that leads over into Miner Canyon."

"There are a lot of tracks that lead into Miner Canyon," Mitchell said. "That doesn't mean anything."

Lassiter nodded. "And it's not Driscoll's tracks alone that made me convinced that he was in with Sloan."

"How do you mean?" Mitchell asked.

"The way the tracks looked, Driscoll was obviously meeting with someone up at that pass," Lassiter pointed out. "There was another horse's tracks mixed with those of Driscoll's horse. Then I followed the trail left by the other horse down the other side and found the cabin."

All of the men on the town council began to talk at once. Some were now very suspicious of Driscoll, while others were taking his side. The room was divided.

"How can you be convinced it was Driscoll you were following?" one of the businessmen asked. "Did you actually *see* Driscoll riding up there?"

"I told you, it was his horse," Lassiter said. "I didn't have to see Driscoll himself."

Again there was more discussion. A number of the men didn't want to take Lassiter's word that he was a good enough tracker to distinguish between the tracks of one horse over those of another. It seemed hard for them to understand that merely watching how a man carries his weight on a horse can determine how the horse leaves tracks.

Lassiter finally realized he wasn't going to convince anyone totally.

"All I'm saying," Lassiter finally told them, "is that we should be watching Mr. Driscoll from now on."

The meeting adjourned and Harold Mitchell was silent for a while as he and Lassiter walked together across the street to the hotel and saloon. Lassiter could see that he was angry, and that he didn't hold with accusing someone without definite proof. But in Lassiter's mind there was positive proof. He just couldn't make anyone else see that.

When they reached the saloon, Mitchell announced that he was going up to join in the poker game, as usual, and that they would discuss the matter of Driscoll the next morning at breakfast. Both Lassiter and Mitchell realized that Driscoll would likely be missing from the poker game this evening.

"It's not good to point fingers at a man like that," Mitchell said. "You're dividing this town in half."

"I have all the proof I need to know that Driscoll is in with Sloan," Lassiter said matter-of-factly.

"Are you absolutely sure that was Driscoll's horse that you were following up that hill?" Mitchell asked.

"I've tracked men and horses all my life," Lassiter said. "Even if Driscoll's horse wasn't shod so that I knew the shoe marks, I could track him just by the way the horse holds his weight. I'm not mistaken."

"So be it," Mitchell said with a nod. "We'll just have to wait and see what happens."

Lassiter watched Mitchell go into the saloon and up the stairway to the poker room. There were a lot of people in the saloon who were now watching him. Some of them eventually turned away and resumed their conversations, and others left the saloon entirely.

After a couple of whiskeys Lassiter became aware of another set of eyes watching him from the top of the stairway. Lassiter looked up and saw Lanna smiling down at him. She moved her body slightly, twisting one shoulder back, as if working to pull him toward her. Lassiter understood that she didn't want to come down into the saloon area.

Lassiter smiled slightly and downed one more whiskey before he walked up the stairs. Lanna had moved off into a small hallway that led to a ballroom. There she awaited him and pretended she had all the time in the world when she wanted in the worst way for him to hurry to her and let her put her arms around his neck. She had kissed him before when there had been a stolen moment. Tonight she knew they would have more time.

When Lassiter reached Lanna, he could see that the broad smile on her face had widened.

"That's a right smart dress," he told her. "Of course, you grace all dresses. That's a fact."

"You're too much, Lassiter," she said. "I don't know how you do it, but you manage to make a lady feel all woman. If you tell my father I said that to you, I'll deny it."

"Your father doesn't care much for what I say anyway," Lassiter told her. "Not when it comes to Driscoll."

"Yes, I understand you made the town council meeting interesting tonight," she said. "Do you really think Driscoll is in with Sloan and his gang?"

"I have no doubt about it," Lassiter said. "I just have to prove it to everyone else. I thought I did that tonight, but no one wants to see the truth."

"You're going to have a hard time convincing my father of that," Lanna said. "He and Driscoll are close friends."

"I know that," Lassiter said. "And that's a problem."

"And I don't think my father is particularly excited about my wanting to be with you."

"Why should he care?" Lassiter said. "You're a grown woman."

"He wants me to take a liking to Driscoll. Can you imagine that?"

"No."

"But I have no intention of doing any such thing."

"Good," Lassiter said. "You're a lady of much more class, and a patient lady as well."

"I'm glad you can see that," Lanna said. "You haven't paid me much mind since that first day. I know you've been busy working for my father, but I was becoming troubled."

"You're not too troubled," Lassiter told her. "I can see that. I was just wondering how you're getting over the loss of your fiancé."

"I've decided I have to go forward with my life," Lanna answered. "I can't dwell on what might have been. I have to work toward the future."

"How long had you known this man?" Lassiter asked.

"Two weeks."

"Two weeks and suddenly it's true love?" Lassiter asked.

Lanna shrugged. "I thought it was. It could have been, you know."

Lassiter nodded. "That's true. My apologies for being out of line."

"I'll forgive you," Lanna said. "But you have to spend more time with me from now on."

"That sound like a good plan to me," Lassiter told her. "It's like you said, I've been busy with your father and the problems this town is facing with the Sloan Gang. But I've noticed you. And I know you've been watching me. I just don't know how good an idea it would be to get to know each other too well. I won't be in Glitter Creek all that long."

"But you're here now," Lanna said. "Let's not worry about tomorrow, or the day after that. I hope you don't think I'm being too forward, but I believe in speaking my mind."

"I like a woman who knows what she wants and goes after it," Lassiter said. "Women aren't supposed to do that. But everyone admires the ones that do. I'm willing to live for today if you are. But just one day at a time."

Lanna put her arm in Lassiter's, and he started for his room. There was little question in Lassiter's mind that Lanna had plans to try and keep him in Glitter Creek. She was a woman who could work her way into and out of things with ease, that was plain. And it was just as plain that she usually got what she wanted. It occurred to him that she would be working hard as the time passed to get him as well.

8

THE STAGE ROLLED TWICE without incident. Two weekends in a row. They carried passengers out of Glitter Creek and on down to Coeur d'Alene, then picked up passengers there and at various points back toward Glitter Creek. Both times a small posse accompanied Lassiter and the driver, and both times the Sloan Gang was nowhere to be seen.

Harold Mitchell was very pleased, and Glitter Creek began to think that Big Jack Sloan and his gang were finished. Lassiter knew very well that Sloan wasn't even close to finished. And the reason that Sloan wasn't hitting the stage was that somehow Driscoll had still been able to meet with Sloan and get information to him.

Lassiter didn't have to think too hard to realize that while he was watching the mines or on the stage runs, Driscoll was going back up to the pass and meeting with Sloan. Lassiter worried that Driscoll was learning a lot about what was going to happen in town from

Harold Mitchell, and then telling it to Sloan. It was all too easy.

Driscoll was playing Harold Mitchell like a honky-tonk piano. He was loaning Mitchell more money now to expand the hotel and saloon into a bigger facility. Mitchell didn't even have to sign any papers. Mitchell was more convinced now that Driscoll was working on his side. And since there had been no more stage holdups for a time, Mitchell was thinking most of the trouble was over.

It was good that Sloan and his gang weren't bothering the stage, but Lassiter knew that wouldn't last much longer. The townspeople, especially Harold Mitchell, were beginning to think now that Lassiter had been wrong by implying that Driscoll had ties with Sloan. Mitchell said it more than once, that he thought Lassiter owed Driscoll an apology. Lassiter told Mitchell that the apology could wait until the Sloan Gang no longer existed. Then he would be collecting some apologies for himself.

As the third weekend of stage runs drew near, Lassiter became aware of the fact that some of the miners in town had banded together to buy some property and livestock down in the valley. They were going to start a large cattle ranching operation to sell beef to the mining towns in the region. They wanted to send a large shipment of their gold on the stage to Coeur d'Alene, where they would finalize the deal for the land.

Between stage runs Lassiter had continued to work for Harold Mitchell out near some of the mines, guarding them against claim jumpers. Lassiter told Mitchell he would be better off hiring someone else to watch for claim jumpers so that he could keep his eyes open for the Sloan Gang. But Harold Mitchell was worried about all the gold that was being brought out; sooner or later someone was bound to try and steal some of it.

Lassiter knew in the back of his mind that the main reason Sloan hadn't hit the stage yet was because Driscoll had been telling him about the posses going with them. Now Sloan was waiting for just the right time to hit the stage once again. And Driscoll would tell him when that time would be.

Driscoll and Sloan were probably both laughing, Lassiter thought. Driscoll had Harold Mitchell right where he wanted him, and Mitchell was without a clue. Lassiter decided it was time to catch Driscoll and show the town once and for all that their banker was worse than any of the outlaws living in Miner Canyon.

He found Lanna coming down the stairway for breakfast the morning before the stage was to leave once again. He was to take the gold over to Coeur d'Alene this time, and he knew it was going to be the time when Sloan and his gang would make a move.

Lassiter walked over to the bottom of the stairs, and Lanna winked at him. He extended his arm for her to take.

"Mr. Lassiter, you're much too serious for a beautiful day like this," she observed.

"I need you to help me with a plan," Lassiter said.

When they were seated and had ordered, Lassiter told her about the gold shipment leaving the next day.

"I think everyone in town knows about that," Lanna said. "What kind of plan do you have?"

"What do you want to bet that Driscoll will tell Sloan about it, and we'll have a holdup tomorrow?"

"Are you still on that?" Lanna asked. "I would have hoped you were convinced of being wrong by now."

"I can see your father has heavy influence over you after all," Lassiter said. "Now I suppose you are going to start letting Driscoll court you."

Lanna's eyes snapped. "I'm not going to do any such thing. I don't even care for the man all that much. But that doesn't mean I think he's an outlaw."

"Let me show you that he is," Lassiter said. "But you have to help me."

"What are you going to do?" Lanna asked.

"I have to prove to your father and the rest of these blind townspeople that Driscoll is in with Sloan," Lassiter said. "After I'm through with him, everyone will see that he's one of them."

Lanna looked hard at him. "If you can prove that, then I'll help you any way I can."

It was late afternoon when Driscoll reached the pass. He had been riding hard, and his horse was nearly played out completely. But he was in a hurry; Lassiter was watching the gold that was being taken from the mines, and he would be snooping around again before long. Driscoll wanted to be back down and in his office before that happened.

Sloan was there waiting for him and mentioned in passing that he had ridden his horse a bit too hard for the rough country.

"You don't have Lassiter watching you all the time!" Driscoll snapped.

Sloan grunted. "He's as good as dead tomorrow. Is that gold shipment going through for sure?"

Now Driscoll was smiling. "They'll be at the bank

to pick it up first thing in the morning. But they're going to have a posse with them again."

"I figured that much," Sloan said. "But they've been turning back at the first station. They'll likely do that again—or have you heard different?"

"No, I haven't heard different," Driscoll said. He was looking around nervously, as if he was worried that Lassiter had followed him. He knew better, but he couldn't help himself.

"I thought you weren't worried about ridin' up here now," Sloan said. "Ain't Lassiter guardin' them mines?"

Driscoll nodded. "But he's a sly one."

"We'll get him tomorrow," Sloan said again. "I just want to be sure that the posse turns back before the first stop."

"I think you can be sure they will," Driscoll said. "I know a lot of them are dropping out, and the rest are getting bored with it. They don't think you're ever going to rob the stage again."

Sloan laughed. "Let them think it."

"I'm going back," Driscoll said. "You should have plenty of time now to figure out how you want to stop the stage when they get down toward the first stop."

"I'll worry about that," Sloan said. "You just worry about tellin' me the right things. That way things will work good on both ends. You just keep ridin' up here every Friday before noon."

"You're forgetting one thing," Driscoll said. "I've got Lassiter to worry about down there. You can't expect me to just ride out of town to see you as bold as you please, like I have before. Like I said, he's been watching me close lately. And I don't want him proving anything to Mitchell. I've got Mitchell in my back pocket right now, and I don't want to lose him."

"I told you already," Sloan said in a growl, "I'm killin' that Lassiter tomorrow. If what you've just said about the gold shipment is right, we'll take care of Lassiter and the gold, too."

"Well, you'd better get him," Driscoll said. "If you don't, there'll be more trouble than we've ever seen before. I can feel it. You had better get him."

"We'll get him," Sloan said. "You just be sure that you can handle things on your end down there. After tomorrow Glitter Creek will be ours."

Driscoll watched Sloan turn his horse and ride back through the pass toward the newly built hideout. It would be nice, Driscoll thought, to have that much confidence in what was going to happen. Driscoll could feel within him that somehow things weren't going to be that easy. Maybe the posse would stick with the stage for once. Even if they didn't, this stranger, Lassiter, was no ordinary shotgun rider. No matter how you looked at him, he was no ordinary man.

When Driscoll got back to town, he noticed Lassiter's horse tied in front of the bank. A lot of things went through Driscoll's mind, including the fear that Lassiter was aware he had just had a meeting with Big Jack Sloan. Driscoll fought the paranoia, rationalizing that it was impossible that Lassiter could have any knowledge about where he had been. Lassiter could have hunches already, but he couldn't have any concrete evidence.

Still, Lassiter's possible presence in the bank bothered Driscoll, and he decided he didn't want to discuss anything with Lassiter right now. But he would need to find something legitimate to be doing with his time. He didn't want it to appear to anyone that he was in town and not at the bank, unless there was good reason for it.

Driscoll decided he could indeed find good reason for not being at the bank. He turned his horse toward the Glitter Creek Hotel. He could find Harold Mitchell and bolster his relationship with him, and his grip on Mitchell's trust. After all, he had lent Mitchell the money to get his hotel started and his mine in operation. So far Mitchell did not know that the money had actually been sent down by Big Jack Sloan—stolen money to finance the Sloan Gang's eventual takeover of Glitter Creek.

Driscoll was smiling while he tied his horse in front of the hotel. He walked through the doors into the lobby, and his stomach began to feel as if it had just dropped down through the floor. Standing in front of him was Lassiter.

"How are you doing, Driscoll?" Lassiter asked, standing over the banker with his arms crossed. "I was just coming over to the bank to see you, but I guess you just saved me the trip."

"Why is your horse over there?" Driscoll wanted to know.

Lassiter smiled. "Lanna is getting ready to go for a ride. She wanted to make some deposits for her father first, so I told her she had just as well do that and wait for me over there. You see, she wanted to talk to you if I missed you."

Driscoll tried to move around Lassiter, but Lassiter stopped him.

"I came in to visit with Harold Mitchell," Driscoll said. "So if you will please pardon me . . ."

"Mr. Mitchell is busy at the moment," Lassiter said. "Besides, I told you I wanted to talk to you. Now, sit down in that chair over there."

"I will do no such thing."

"Do you want me to help you sit down?" Lassiter asked. "It might be embarrassing. People are already beginning to stare."

Driscoll blew out his breath and moved over to one of the chairs. Lassiter sat down in one nearby and told Driscoll right away that the gold was being delayed for a week.

Driscoll tried to hide his surprise, but Lassiter was quick to see his expression.

"Why does that bother you, Driscoll?" Lassiter asked. "Why should it make any difference to you when the gold goes out?"

"Well, I spent considerable time planning for it to go out tomorrow is all," Driscoll finally managed. He worked at his tie while he spoke, looking as if he might hang himself with it if he wasn't careful.

"I see," Lassiter said. "The gold is resting in the vault in bags. What more would you have to do?"

Driscoll's face was red. "Listen," he finally said, "I don't have to sit here and be questioned by you. Good day."

As Driscoll started to get up, Lassiter warned him. It caught Driscoll in the act of rising and held him there, half out of the chair.

"As soon as I can prove you're tied in with these stage holdups," Lassiter said, "I'll find the biggest tree I can find and watch the townspeople hang you. Then you won't need a necktie anymore. Do you understand me, Driscoll?"

Driscoll's eyes were huge. He straightened up as

Lassiter rose from the chair next to him and walked past him, then out the door, without ever looking back.

When Lassiter was out the door, Driscoll caught his breath and readjusted his tie. He still couldn't breathe very well, and his nerves seemed to be on fire. What was he going to do now? He couldn't tell Sloan there was no gold shipment going out—Lassiter would be watching him. There was nothing he could do but let things happen as they might.

Driscoll managed to make his way out the door of the hotel. He hesitated to see if Lassiter was anywhere in sight. When he decided the street was clear, he started toward the bank.

Partway to the bank Driscoll stopped in the street and stared as he watched Lanna walk out of the bank with Lassiter and then climb on the big sorrel. She rode off and Lassiter walked over toward another part of town without once looking his way.

Driscoll went the rest of the way to the bank and walked inside. Everyone said hello and hoped he had had a good trip to the little towns to see about banks being needed there. Everything seemed normal. But it wasn't. The stranger named Lassiter was in town. And if Sloan and his gang didn't kill this stranger the next day, Driscoll knew in his own mind his plan was going to backfire.

9

THERE WAS A ROLL of thunder and suddenly Glitter Creek was doused with a summer-morning thundershower. Lassiter finished his breakfast while passengers getting ready to board the stage gathered inside the lobby of the hotel. There were a number of men carrying rifles and leading their horses across the street toward the hotel. They began to run with their horses and, after they had hitched them, joined the others inside.

The men and the stage passengers watched outside while water dripped from the stage and down off the eaves of the buildings. It was a sudden mountain cloudburst common here this time of year. The water usually came in a hurry and it was over with. Today was no exception, as there suddenly came a letup in the rain and a rainbow appeared just over the mountain.

Lassiter watched the passengers begin to chatter among themselves. He wanted to be as vibrant as they were, but he was sensitive to the fact that the day might hold danger for the passengers and everyone else riding the stage. This run in particular had him worried. It was not so much the gold as it was the timing—the way things were starting to shape up. The men in the posse were already talking about what they wanted to do when they got back. That meant they weren't going to be riding with the stage that long this time.

Lassiter continued to think about what might happen. The run could go smooth, but likely not. He was sure that Big Jack Sloan wanted revenge as soon as he could get it, and he wanted to get Glitter Creek as fast as he could as well. The summer was ending, and soon the snow would come to the higher country and stop the stage runs. Sloan wouldn't want to have to wait through the winter.

There was another reason Lassiter was sure of trouble. As usual, Gil Driscoll was acting jumpy and nervous. He hadn't been able to get out of town to tell Driscoll that there was to be no gold shipment. Lassiter knew without question Driscoll had taken the bait and actually believed the gold had been delayed. This meant he was worried that Sloan would be jumping a stage with no gold and would blame him for it.

"A penny for your thoughts. . . ."

Lassiter looked up to see Lanna standing beside the table, smiling warmly.

Lassiter rose from his seat. "Excuse me, Lanna," he said. "I guess I wasn't paying much attention to things."

Lanna took a seat across from Lassiter as he pulled a chair out for her. She was dressed in her black gingham dress. She hadn't worn it since the day of the stage holdup. Lassiter thought she looked as striking in it today as when he had first met her.

"That was quite a little rainstorm we just had," she commented.

"It will freshen the air," Lassiter said.

A waiter came over and poured Lanna some coffee. She sipped at it for a few moments. It seemed to Lassiter that she was concerned about something.

"It looks like you will have a lot of passengers for this trip," Lanna commented. "Are you worried about Sloan and his gang?"

"Yes," Lassiter answered. "I don't know what to expect up there. But I would say trouble is waiting."

Lanna turned to watch the activity in the lobby for a moment, then turned back to Lassiter.

"Are those men from town that just came in with rifles going with the stage?"

"There is a small posse going up as far as the first stage stop, as usual," Lassiter said. "I just hope they don't decide to turn back before then."

"I guess there is no real hope in thinking that Sloan will quit robbing my father's stage line, even though you shot his men up so badly," Lanna said.

Lassiter shook his head. "I don't think there's any hope in that at all. Men like Sloan don't often think rationally. They operate strictly by emotion—and that emotion is usually anger."

"If you can kill Sloan, will our troubles be over?"

Lassiter thought a moment. It was a good question, but it depended entirely on whether or not there was another member of the gang who could lead them. If that someone existed, then killing Sloan would only bring that man to the surface.

"Sloan won't be easy to kill," Lassiter finally said.

"And if he is killed somehow, it doesn't necessarily mean there aren't more road agents where he came from."

"Why don't you just take a posse of men up into the mountains and find Sloan and his men?" Lanna asked. "Just find them and hang them all."

"It's not that simple," Lassiter said. "First of all, we would have to have someone along who could positively identify Sloan. He would have to know Sloan cold—no guessing. When you start guessing, you can hang the wrong people."

"There must be somebody who would know him," Lanna said. "Surely somebody has seen him."

"It's better if he comes and is caught in the act of stealing or attempting to steal," Lassiter said. "That way there is no question what is going on, no guessing."

"Do you think Sloan expects to find gold on the stage?" Lanna asked.

"I know he does," Lassiter answered. "I'm certain Driscoll told him about the gold. And when I told Driscoll the shipment was going to be delayed, he went crazy."

Lanna looked over her cup of coffee at Lassiter. She could now see the logic in setting Gil Driscoll up. Sloan was going after the stage expecting to find gold, as Driscoll had told him. If Lassiter had allowed Driscoll to sneak out of town after he told him the gold shipment had been delayed, the chances were good that Sloan wouldn't attack the stage.

"So you're certain that Gil Driscoll is trying to turn this town over to the Sloan Gang?" Lanna asked.

"As certain as the day is long," Lassiter answered with a nod. "But I want him to show his hand to your father and everyone in this town by himself. I'll keep setting him up this way and sooner or later, he'll break."

"Sometimes I think you're too calculating," Lanna said. "You keep your feet on the ground, don't you?"

"A man like me has to," Lassiter said. "You can get yourself killed if you jump into water and don't check for rocks first."

Lanna noticed her father coming in, and within moments he joined them at the table. He was visibly nervous and wondered why Lassiter appeared so calm.

"There are only so many things that can happen up there," Lassiter said. "I've thought about them for a while; now we just have to wait and see what Sloan does."

"Surely he won't attempt to rob the stage with the posse along guarding it," Mitchell said.

"I think you're right," Lassiter agreed. "But it all depends on how crazy Sloan is for revenge. He might come on anyway and just try to blast us all up. Or he might think better of it and wait for another day. It's hard to say."

Mitchell drummed his fingers against the table. "I just don't like it—all this waiting."

"Just think of it this way," Lassiter said. "Sloan's feeling the same way, only he's got something to prove now. That puts the pressure on him."

Mitchell nodded. "I guess you're right. There's no sense in us getting all tense when Sloan is the one who has to save face now."

Big Jack Sloan settled his horse down and pulled himself up into the saddle. He had just finished whipping the horse into a lather of sweat and fear, something he did to his horse just before each ride out to rob and kill.

Macey had heard Sloan's explanation for the way he treated his horse before, and he knew better. Macey knew it was a way for Sloan to exert his authority, to show the others in the gang that they could be whipped if they didn't stay in line. He especially wanted to show something to the newcomers, Coleman and the kid, Donny Jenks. This was their first job with the gang, and Sloan wanted them to be sure they knew who was giving the orders.

Macey watched Sloan and his little ritual with the horse, as he had each time they were going out to rob. He would watch while Sloan whipped the horse with the reins and cursed and got himself enraged so that his face was beet red. Today, as he did each time, he got on the horse and reined it around roughly with the bridle, tearing at its mouth with the bit.

Most of the gang didn't watch, for most thought more of horses than that. Donny Jenks hadn't watched any of it from the beginning. But Coleman was watching like he enjoyed it. And it was getting him primed for the holdup as well.

Macey and the others couldn't understand why Sloan treated his horse like he did. Sloan's horse would run away from him every chance it got. Horses got you around in this country, and they could mean life or death if you were stranded a long way from a settlement. For that reason it had always amazed Macey that no one stepped forward to protest. But the reality was, everyone in the gang was afraid of Sloan. He was as merciless with everyone else as he was with his horse.

The same tricks had worked on Macey for a time, and he realized it. But now he was thinking. Maybe there was something more to the way Sloan acted with his horse than just mere intimidation.

Macey hadn't given it much thought before, but it was slowly coming to light that Sloan needed a crutch of some kind to get himself hyped up for each of the jobs. He beat his horses to show how heartless he was, but he also beat them to get himself ready for the job.

This seemed odd to Macey, for it seemed the thrill of the act itself would be all someone would need to get himself into the right frame of mind. Robbing and shooting people was what Macey lived for, and he assumed the same of Big Jack Sloan. Perhaps that wasn't altogether true.

Macey finally began to realize that possibly the stranger was making Sloan more nervous than usual. There was something about this Lassiter that made everyone more attentive about getting ready for the job. It seemed as if nothing scared the man, no large odds against him or anything of that sort. He was going to be hard to bring down.

But Sloan wanted him bad, and this was the day. Going after the gold seemed secondary to Sloan at this time. Something told Macey that Sloan was getting more and more worried about Lassiter and was possibly losing confidence. To Macey's way of thinking, this was a bad time to have that happen.

The ride out of Miner Canyon was silent. They were headed for the end of a high plateau where the Mullen Road worked its way down out of the timber and onto the valley bottom. There was a stage stop located at the bottom of the steep grade up onto the top. Sloan had planned it so that the stage wouldn't make it that far.

During the past two runs the posse had been leaving the stage just a mile or two from the stop. The stage had gone the rest of the way down out of the timber and onto the bottom with just Lassiter to make sure things were safe. From there on the country was open, and road agents had little chance of getting close to a stage without being seen from a good distance.

"You all know what to do," Sloan said to everyone when they reached a thick grove of timber just before the road broke off toward the bottom. "Let's get it done fast."

The men took to chopping down a large tree with an ax. It would fall down across the stage road and block it. There were rocks on both sides of the road, and no way for the stage to go around the tree. The stage would have to stop.

"That would give Mr. Lassiter some trouble," Sloan said as he watched the tree being chopped.

The others in the gang agreed, and some of them began laughing. They took turns chopping while the others checked their guns to be sure they were loaded and ready to fire. One of the gang members was just sitting his horse and wasn't looking his weapons over.

"What's the matter, Jenks?" Sloan asked the kid. "You'd better get ready. That stage is due any time."

"I don't want any part of this anymore," Jenks then said. "I've never wanted any part of this. I'm going to just ride away from this and leave it all behind me."

The chopping stopped and everyone stared. They watched Sloan look at the kid as if he couldn't believe what he had just heard. As Jenks began to turn his horse, Sloan pulled his own horse around and rode in front of the kid.

"What the hell are you talking about?" Sloan said. "You can't just ride off like that."

"Please move your horse, Mr. Sloan," Jenks said. "I want to get by."

"No, you're not getting by," Sloan said. "I should have done this the first day."

Sloan then pulled his pistol and fired twice. The kid jerked in the saddle as the bullets struck him in the lower chest and stomach area. He fell from the horse and rolled sideways into a ball. Sloan pulled the hammer back once again and aimed down at Jenks.

The bullet took Jenks in the head, just behind the right ear. The kid jumped as if he had been kicked and then tensed up and jerked for a time before relaxing and lying still. Everyone was staring at Sloan now, all of them in shock. They had all seen men die before, but not like this.

"That kid wasn't goin' to be able to make it," Coleman finally said. "I just knew he wasn't."

Sloan turned to Coleman and his lips curled. "Shut up!" he growled. "I ain't sure if you're right for this bunch yet, either."

"Look, I'll do anything you say, Mr. Sloan," Coleman said. He had his hands raised like he thought Sloan was going to raise the pistol and shoot him as well. "Listen, I'll do anything."

"I said shut up!" Sloan yelled. He was staring hard at Coleman, working his thumb over the hammer of his revolver. Finally he turned to the others, who were staring. "Get that tree down," he said. "If it ain't down by the time that stage gets here, I'll kill you all."

10

THE STAGE CREAKED ALONG the rutted wagon trail that was the Mullen Road. The sun was already nearing mid-sky, and the smell of summer pine was strong, owing to the thundershower of the night before. It was a strong day and, in Lassiter's mind, too good of a day to last.

Even though there was a posse riding with them for a distance out of town, Lassiter felt that the men should stay with them until they got down off the mountain ridges and into the lower country. But that would be too far for them, and they would have to turn back after the first stop.

Most everyone agreed the first stop was well beyond the Sloan Gang territory anyway—everyone except Lassiter.

The posse rode along with the stage, and the men talked about getting back to Glitter Creek. They were well past the area where the Sloan Gang usually hit the stage, if a robbery was to occur. Neither Lassiter

93

nor the driver was happy about it when the posse finally left them, just two miles before the first stop.

The bench where they now rode was open, except for certain places where the road forged its way through rock and timber. Lassiter talked to the driver about the gold boom in the territory and how news of the various strikes was reaching far and wide, bringing people in droves. The thought of instant wealth was a fever that could never be cured.

But the discussion did not take the driver's mind off the peril of driving with a load of gold and nobody but one shotgun rider to protect everyone. The driver was spitting tobacco nervously. He had never met Lassiter, and he was sure Lassiter could do more than most men, but it would be impossible to stand off as many men as the Sloan Gang would throw at them.

Lassiter could see out across the country, over the jutting expanse of timbered mountains that rose in the vast distance to snowy peaks. Travel here was restricted to bottoms along the rivers and streams or occasionally along the top where the traveling was easier than down in the thick timber and rock of the hillsides.

It was easy to see why this country was good for thieves. Cover was abundant and the ability to escape on horseback after a robbery was unlimited. As more people came into the territory to look for gold, gangs like Big Jack Sloan's would become more prominent. It was important to keep these gangs from enjoying early success—the better they did initially, the more confidence they gained. That made it harder to stop them.

The jolting stage rocked its way along the road, and Lassiter moved with the rhythm, his rifle balanced across his knees. A big twelve-gauge shotgun, double-barreled, rested atop the stage just behind the seat. It would be there if needed, but Lassiter's philosophy was that rifles were good for long range and shotguns were best for close-up work. You could finish things with a scattergun in good order, but if you waited for a man to get into range, it might already be too late.

The passengers on the trip seemed to be more concerned with the rough ride than the danger of Big Jack Sloan and his gang. Six people were inside the stage—two women and their husbands, plus a gambler and a young soldier reporting to duty at Fort Coeur d'Alene. He wore a big Colt Navy revolver on his left side and had been watching Lassiter closely ever since the stage left that morning. He was young and he was looking for action. He knew Lassiter had seen plenty of it.

Lassiter could tell that the kid was just itching to ask him what it was like to be a gunfighter. Something in the kid's eyes told Lassiter he wanted to use a gun well and have people look up to him for it. What the kid didn't understand was that people didn't look up to you in the sense that they respected you; they looked up to you with fear. The fact of the matter was they really didn't look at you any more than they had to, for fear of angering you. The life of a gunman was a lonely one indeed.

What Lassiter wanted to tell the kid and would, if the kid should ask, was that getting into the life of a gunman was a wrong move. By accident or on purpose, shooting for a living made you a slave to the trade—it never let you go. Until the day you died, you were branded a gunfighter.

By comparison, the gambler was a slinky, conniving

sort who stole glances at Lassiter but would never look him in the eye. He was of the sort who would plant a knife in your back should the opportunity arise and should there be a few dollars in the action. Otherwise, his type contented themselves with taking money via a card game from unsuspecting and drunk cowhands at the end of the trailheads, or possibly soldiers on leave with a month's pay to surrender to either a woman or a card game.

The two men and their wives seemed ignorant to either the gambler or the kid with the big Colt. They had fashioned an idea of going out from Glitter Creek and gathering support from relatives on the West Coast to open a large dry goods store in town. They wanted to bring in all kinds of supplies not readily available in mining camps and other remote locations.

They realized boomtowns like Glitter Creek held patrons with ready cash who wanted to spend it fast on the first thing that caught their fancy. In addition, clothing and other housewares were a necessity, and the finer the quality the more apt people were to invest in the goods.

It was in the back of Lassiter's mind that all of these people were lost in their own small world, sitting in the stage and daydreaming the bumpy miles away, not once wondering if their lives might not end before the sun set that night. They had not even bothered to put up a fuss when the posse had deserted them not far back. They were all concerned about getting to their destinations.

People had so many plans, and no way of understanding that they might never come to pass. Lassiter had always felt better off living the days as they went by, drifting with his notions and earning his dollars a few at a time. They were always there, and it was a lot easier not having to worry about collecting great heaps of them all at once, just so someone else could try and take them away from you.

They were just a mile from the first stop now. The day was bright, and ordinarily the warm sun would have made Lassiter relax. But under the circumstances there was little way he could keep from being alert every moment. It seemed to him that Sloan would be out to teach Harold Mitchell a lesson. Now would be the opportune time to do that, for this was the first stage run after what had happened up here on the hill a week past.

Sloan would be thinking that he should stop this run and therefore set a precedent that he indeed owned the Mullen Road. With only a small distance of timber left ahead of them, Lassiter was sure that Sloan had hoped to lull him to sleep. Instead, Lassiter was even more aware, and he told the driver to slow the team and stop.

"What's the matter?" the driver asked. "I don't see nothing." He spat a wad of tobacco.

Lassiter pointed up to where the road worked its way through the last heavy grove of trees and rocks.

"You see a downed tree across the trail up there?" Lassiter asked.

The driver squinted. "Right near that rock by the trail," he said.

"That's it," Lassiter said with a nod. He checked his rifle. "Let's just wait here and see what happens."

The driver held the horses, and the passengers began to look out the window, wondering why they had stopped. Lassiter told them to keep their heads inside and wait until he said different. The young kid with the Colt Navy looked out one of the windows again and shouted up to Lassiter.

"I'll get up there and help you," he said. "If there's thieves, we can stand them off."

"Stay put," Lassiter said. "This won't be no picnic up here."

Lassiter sat atop the stage with the driver and watched the trees up ahead where the road came around the rock. The tree that had been cut and hauled across the road was obviously meant to stop the stage. Big Jack Sloan and his gang had to be waiting in the trees. By now Sloan and his bunch would know that the stage was stopped out in the open. Lassiter figured that Sloan was by now mad as a wet hen.

"Maybe that tree just got blowed down by the wind," the driver said, putting more tobacco into his mouth.

Lassiter shook his head. "Not a chance."

"I don't see nobody," the driver said.

"They're trying to wait us out," Lassiter said. "But there are no trees near enough to us for them to come up and ambush us from. We've got all the time in the world."

After a time of waiting the driver began to get nervous. "What do you figure is going to happen up there?" the driver asked Lassiter.

Lassiter was smiling. "It seems to me that Big Jack Sloan is now looking at his whole hand of cards. My guess is he's in too deep now to fold. He'll come out after us and it won't be long."

"I don't care to be up here in the line of fire when they come," the driver said.

"You just hold the horses," Lassiter said. "I'll do

the shooting. If we work together, we all get out of this alive."

The driver spat more tobacco. "I'm figuring on you for your word."

"Good," Lassiter said. "Take a tight hold on those reins now, 'cause here they come."

Riders were emerging from the trees with their guns drawn, spurring their horses toward the stagecoach. They were fanning out as they came, in order to get out and surround the stage from three directions. Lassiter knew he had to start shooting now or it would be too late.

Lassiter stood up and braced himself. He aimed at the first rider starting away from the main group and fired. The thief pitched backward from the saddle, and the others spread out even more, with Sloan yelling at them to keep going.

Lassiter levered another round into the barrel and aimed at the first rider branching out on the other side. Again there was a sharp crack, and the rider toppled sideways, his boot catching in the stirrup. The horse dragged him away yelling.

Confusion and fear began to grip Sloan's men. None of them wanted to be the next victim of Lassiter's rifle. Lassiter could see that Sloan's men wanted to give up the fight. They looked to Sloan for direction, holding their horses up, and Sloan was yelling, waving for them to come ahead with him. Lassiter got his rifle ready again and noticed that the kid was getting out of the stagecoach.

"I said stay inside!" Lassiter yelled down at him.

"I ain't letting you get all of them yourself," the kid

yelled back. He pulled his big Colt and began fanning it wildly in the direction of Sloan and his gang.

Sloan and his men were closing in on the stage now, and Lassiter cursed the luck. Had he ignored the kid and just started shooting again, it was likely he could have headed the gang off before they got close. Now it was too late.

Sloan and his gang pressed past the stage, pouring bullets from their guns. Lead thumped into the wood of the stage and one bullet sang off the iron railing at Lassiter's feet. Inside, the women were screaming and the men were yelling. Outside, the kid was getting riddled with bullets.

The kid had emptied his Colt before the gang reached the stage and was reloaded when they opened up on him. He spun with the first volley and fell against the stage, sagging as they rode past, leaving a wide smear of blood against the stage door as he slumped to the ground.

Lassiter fired his rifle over the cursing driver as the driver fought to control the horses. Before, the horses had been easy to manage and Lassiter had had little trouble in aiming and remaining still. But now the stage was jolting, and Lassiter's shots were hit-and-miss.

As Sloan and his men turned in the road for another rush at the stage, Lassiter jumped down to the ground and dropped to one knee. He could see the thieves getting set behind Sloan for the charge, and he knew that if he didn't make each shot count, there would be no tomorrow.

Sloan led the rush and Lassiter waited. Sloan saw Lassiter's rifle aimed at him and turned his horse just as the smoke puffed from the barrel. Sloan's horse squealed and jumped in one motion, but did not move fast enough to keep Sloan from getting hit.

The bullet tore into Sloan's leg at the top of his left knee. Blood and bone fragments flew up along his leg and coated the side of his horse. Sloan screamed and clutched both the saddle horn and his horse's mane to keep from falling. He let his horse carry him off the road and down into the trees along the slope.

Lassiter jacked the empty shell out and got ready to fire once more. But he lowered the rifle. It didn't matter now; all the rest of Sloan's men were down off the trail and into the timber. It was plain they were done fighting for the time being. What Lassiter was wondering was if Sloan was finished robbing this road now, or would he be back some other time.

If it hadn't been for the circumstances of the stage and the passengers and the dead kid, Lassiter might have pursued the gang and made sure Sloan was either finished or had surrendered to be brought back to Glitter Creek to answer to the townspeople. But that wasn't possible. The women were still screaming, and the driver was still having trouble handling the horses. The kid was under the wheels, his Colt lying in the grass just off the trail.

Lassiter helped get the horses under control from the ground. He got the women to settle down and told them there was no use for a lot of emotion now— Sloan and his men were gone and they wouldn't be back.

He then went to the kid and brought him out from under the stage. He was dead and there wasn't anything that could change that now. He had wanted to be a soldier. He had wanted to get himself into fights.

He had found his first real fight which turned out to be his last one.

"I suggest we get this stage rolling," the gambler said, hanging his head out the window. "I have places to go."

"We have a dead man here we have to take care of," Lassiter said.

"That is not my concern," the gambler said.

"Well, it is my concern," Lassiter said. "And you're just going to have to live with it."

"Listen," the gambler persisted, "I am in a hurry to get going. I insist we leave now."

Lassiter walked to the stage door and opened it. The gambler watched him, his eyes growing wider as he saw Lassiter's anger.

"Get out," Lassiter said.

"I beg your pardon?"

"I said get out," Lassiter repeated. "Do it now."

The gambler stepped out of the stage and stood in front of Lassiter. He tried to act dignified and worked to straighten his suit. But he was too afraid. He realized he shouldn't have opened his mouth.

"If you're in such a hurry to leave," Lassiter said, "then leave."

"What do you mean?" the gambler asked. "I can't just walk."

Lassiter looked hard at the gambler. He should make this man walk out of this country, find his own way if he was so insolent as to be oppressive at a time like this. But Lassiter realized he might run into Sloan's gang and be killed.

"I'll give you one more chance," Lassiter said. "You get back onto that stage and keep your mouth shut, you can ride on with us. But one more word and you're out. Understand?"

The gambler nodded nervously. He got back in the coach and sat with his eyes averted from everyone. Then Lassiter turned back to the dead kid, wondering if his folks would care that his grave was soon to be located at a lonely stage stop in Idaho Territory.

11

Big Jack Sloan fell from his horse. He remembered trying to turn himself as he fell so that he would land on his back, but he didn't get turned enough and took the fall on his left arm and shoulder—and the knee that was shot to pieces.

Sloan remembered screaming and bouncing. There was the searing heat of pain that exploded up from his knee to engulf his entire body as waves of blackness worked to overcome him. The blackness boiled and he fought it, working at the same time to gain control of his body, which seemed to be moving against his will.

He remembered the sensation of being out of control, rolling downward along the steep slope, atop rocks and small branches and other debris under the trees. It was a momentum that took him along whether or not he wanted to go. It continued to pull him downward, rolling, with an incredible pain that spread from his knee throughout his entire body.

He could sense the blackness in his head trying to

drag him into unconsciousness. He remembered fighting the blackness and then the sudden jolt as the big tree stopped him. He remembered spitting dead pine needles from his lips. Then the blackness won out.

Macey had his pistol drawn and was watching uphill as he made his way to Sloan. The others were up near the top, hoping that the stranger in black didn't come into the trees after them. They were hard-pressed to stay put as it was, wondering if their turn to get shot was coming. But Macey had yelled long and hard enough at them, and they were staying put until he said different.

Sloan's knee was a mess, and Macey was wondering how he was going to get him up and out of the trees. It didn't appear that Sloan was bleeding all that badly, but the bone and tendon damage in the knee seemed immense. Sloan wasn't moving now—he wasn't even groaning anymore—and Macey was wondering what to do.

Finally he decided to call two of the men down to help him get Sloan up out of the trees. If they could get him back up without running into trouble from the stranger, they could tie him to his horse and get him back to the hideout in fairly short order. It was that stranger that Macey was worried about.

While he and the other two worked to get Sloan up the hill, Macey thought about what had happened on top. It had been hard enough getting the tree chopped down and dragged out into the roadway. It had seemed like a bad place to put it, where someone coming could see it from a good distance. But Sloan had argued that the trees were thickest there along the trail, and there were rocks to hide them.

Once the stage had stopped, there was little question they should have decided to quit and try again some other day. Macey could remember that stranger in black pointing from the stagecoach and levering a round into his Winchester. Macey had said repeatedly they should try again when they could catch the stranger by surprise. But, no, Sloan wasn't going to listen to any of that. He had called Macey yellow and had said they were stopping that stage one way or another.

Now Sloan was on the ground with a blasted knee, and there still wasn't any dead stranger dressed in black. Instead there were more of the gang dead. There wasn't enough of them left now to scare a bunch of schoolchildren.

"Check over the ridge and see if the stage is still there," Macey told Coleman.

Sloan had almost killed this man, and as a result Coleman had tried to prove his worth during the shooting. Coleman was lucky Lassiter hadn't gotten him when he was shooting up the young kid in front of the stage. Coleman had wanted to go after Lassiter when Lassiter had wounded Sloan, but Macey had stopped him. He was wondering if he would live to regret that someday.

"We going after them again?" Coleman asked.

"No," Macey answered. "I just want to know if the stage is still there so I can make some decisions. Go up there and look, now. Do it quick!"

Coleman rode off and didn't look back. He was doing what he was told. Coleman and the others didn't seem to question that with Sloan hurt, Macey was now in command. It gave him a rush of power and made him think he could be a better leader of this bunch than Sloan ever thought of being. It suited him a lot better than listening to Sloan. And since the men seemed to respond to him, he could consider himself the leader if Sloan ended up dying.

While Coleman went up the ridge, Macey and the others got Sloan onto his horse and tied him on with lengths of rope. Sloan would slip in and out of consciousness while the men worked, groaning in pain and babbling incoherently. He began to shake and vomit, then finally hung motionless from the horse.

"Do you figure he's dead?" one of the thieves asked Macey.

"I don't think so," Macey said. "But he ain't far from it."

Coleman returned from the hill. "I don't think anybody's coming up here after us," he said. "The passengers are inside the stage, and that stranger is knelt down over that soldier that jumped out of the stage." He began to laugh. "He's just kneeling down there. I guess he figures he can't do nothing for them now. Maybe we should try and take him. What do you say?"

Macey thought about it. He finally decided it wasn't a good idea. Lassiter would be steaming mad, and he would be shooting just as straight as he always did. Besides, it was better to get Sloan back to the hideout and taken care of before he died. Until he found out where that gold was buried, Macey didn't want Sloan dying on him. But if he ever found out, then he just might finish Sloan himself.

"I think we'd better leave well enough alone for now," Macey finally told Coleman. "We've lost enough men for today."

"We could get them," Coleman said. "What about the gold?"

"We're shot up too bad!" Macey yelled. "Or can't you see that?"

"What about the gold?"

"There will be more gold shipments," Macey said. "Right now we've got to get ourselves out of here before Lassiter decides to come down here."

"You're afraid of one man?" Coleman asked.

Macey looked at Coleman as if he couldn't believe what he was hearing. Coleman was actually more stupid than Macey had first thought.

"Coleman, you go right back up there and you get Lassiter," Macey said. "Go right ahead."

"Ain't you and the others comin' with me?" Coleman asked.

"Why should we? You're not afraid to face Lassiter yourself, are you?"

Coleman shrugged. "I was figurin' on all of us."

"I said no!" Macey told him once again. "You go if you want to, but we're not. You either go over the hill and get Lassiter, or stay here with us and shut up. Which is it?"

Coleman shrugged again. "I'll stay."

Macey looked to one of the other men. "I'm going to take Sloan back to the cabin," he said. "And Coleman is coming with me. I want you to take the rest of the men and get down into Glitter Creek and talk to Gil Driscoll. Do it quiet like. Have him tell you where the doctor is, and then you blindfold that doctor and get him back up here. Understand?"

"I'll go with them," Coleman said.

"You'll go with me, or end up like Jenks did," Macey said. "Understand?"

Coleman nodded. He watched while the other road agent took the rest of the gang with him and rode toward Glitter Creek. Macey took Coleman and they led Sloan's horse toward the hideout and stayed to the back trails, watching all the time for any signs that the stranger was trailing them. That was unlikely, since there were people aboard the stage he would have to watch over.

And there was burying to do, a lot of it. That stranger had accounted for a lot of the gang already—enough to make it necessary to try and recruit even more men. They couldn't control the Mullen Road and take over Glitter Creek with what men they now had. It would take some time to get more men, but they would have to be found.

Macey neared the hideout, thinking that things might be looking up for him. Sloan was going to be laid up for a long time with his bad knee. He wouldn't be able to give many orders. Macey would be giving most of them, plus looking out for more men to take into the gang. These men would be loyal to him, though it would take some work to keep Coleman in line. Macey was thinking it wouldn't be long until he essentially had control of the gang himself.

It didn't matter if that didn't suit Sloan. He was in bad shape now, and if he lived, he would have to be grateful. Macey figured Sloan would have to give him credit for getting the doctor up to work on his knee, and he would have to just sit and let that knee rest while Macey led the men around the territory.

But it wouldn't be easy. Macey realized he would have to do his planning carefully. He would have to get all the men with him—including Coleman—before he took full control of the gang. There would have to be a number of successful holdups staged around the area so that the confidence factor built back up again. Lassiter had blown a number of big holes in the gang's confidence.

It occurred to Macey that they should leave the stages along the Mullen Road alone for a while. As long as Lassiter was riding shotgun, there would be little chance of stopping the stages. Perhaps in time he would leave; or perhaps in time he would become overconfident and make a mistake. Time would tell there. But Macey had time on his side.

Lassiter unhitched the team and tied them to the tree. Before long it was off the road and out of the way. The stage passengers were silent as they rolled on to the first stop and waited a while for the change of horses. Lassiter helped the driver harness the fresh horses and feed the team that had brought them through the mountains. It was a good team and well trained, or there would have been runaways during the shooting up on top. Lassiter gave them extra oats.

Lassiter noticed the gambler staring at him off and on, looking at him with hard glances and fingering his pocket, where Lassiter knew a Derringer was concealed. It occurred to Lassiter that the gambler was something more than just the normal tinhorn passing through. There was something about the man that made Lassiter feel uneasy, as if the man knew him or about him.

When the horses were finally cared for, Lassiter found a shovel and helped the driver lower the young man's body from the top of the stage. He had died much too young, and Lassiter couldn't get over how the kid had been trying to help him stand off Sloan and his gang. Now the kid couldn't help anybody do anything ever again.

Everyone but Lassiter and the driver went inside to wait while Lassiter dug a grave for the young would-be soldier.

"I can help you with that," the driver offered.

"I can handle it," Lassiter said. "It gives me time to think."

"It weren't your fault," the driver said.

"I should have kept shooting," Lassiter said, without looking up from his work.

The driver watched him finish the hole and then helped him lower the body, draped in an old saddle blanket.

"I'm sorry, kid," Lassiter said. He began filling the grave and worked steadily until it was covered over and rocks were piled on top. He then placed a crude wooden cross in front.

"He was young and he shouldn't have got out of the coach," the driver told Lassiter. "You told him as much."

"I know," Lassiter said. "But I should've kept shooting."

The passengers reboarded the stage, and Lassiter kept his eye on the gambler throughout the rest of the run to Coeur d'Alene. The stage driver said little throughout the trip, watching Lassiter closely and spitting his tobacco frequently. Finally he asked Lassiter if anyone who argued with him was safe.

That brought a laugh from Lassiter, and the stage driver finally loosened up.

"There's a lot of people who don't agree with me on things," Lassiter said. "That doesn't mean I carry a grudge against them. In fact, I usually argue the most with the people I like the best.''

''Hell, that's good to hear,'' the driver said. '' 'Cause I got two things to say to you.''

''Fire away,'' Lassiter said.

''First off,'' the driver began, ''you stop blamin' yourself for that kid's death. He got outta the coach and that's that. You couldn't do nothin'.''

''What else?'' Lassiter wanted to know.

The driver cleared his throat and spit tobacco again. ''I think you should've put that gambler out on the road and let him walk.''

''Sloan's bunch has killed enough men as it is,'' Lassiter said. ''One more tinhorn gambler wouldn't make a difference to them.''

''He ain't just one more tinhorn gambler,'' the driver said. ''He's a bad one and he's up to somethin' that ain't good.''

''There are a lot of gamblers like him,'' Lassiter said. ''They always make their way to boomtowns.''

''I don't care for the likes of him,'' the driver said. ''I've seen him around Coeur d'Alene a lot. He hangs around with that banker, Gil Driscoll, when he's in town. Driscoll rides over here at times, you know.''

Lassiter turned to the driver. ''Did you say that gambler is a friend of Gil Driscoll's?''

''Don't know if he's a friend or not,'' the driver answered, ''but he spends a lot of time with him.''

Lassiter began to wonder what connection the gambler had with Driscoll. The gambler had no doubt been to Glitter Creek to see Driscoll about something and was now on his way back to Coeur d'Alene. Lassiter concluded that if the gambler was tied in with Driscoll, he also had to be tied in with the Sloan Gang.

Lassiter shifted himself on the seat. It was time to have a discussion with that gambler. Something was going on here, and he intended to find out what it was.

12

LASSITER CONTINUED TO THINK about the gambler's
connection to Driscoll and possible connection with
the Sloan Gang. Lassiter had now determined that it
was unlikely the gambler had connections with the
gang and that the Sloan Gang probably didn't know
anything about the gambler and his link to Driscoll. It
was possible that Driscoll was planning something else
with the gambler that the Sloan Gang had no notion
of. That would be something to look into, Lassiter
thought, just as soon as the stage hit Coeur d'Alene.

Coeur d'Alene was a small town nestled against a
beautiful mountain lake. The new fort was just being
built and the streets were bustling with people. Freight
wagons jammed parts of the town, and a chorus of
honky-tonk music and laughter rolled from the many
saloons.

Lassiter noticed that the gambler got his baggage
and quickly sneaked off so that he didn't have to be
around Lassiter. He had been watching Lassiter from

the corners of his eyes, and the feeling Lassiter had was that the gambler might be planning something.

When all the people were gone from the stage stop, Lassiter began to search for the gambler. He knew the man would likely be looking for a card game from which to cheat his day's earnings.

Lassiter picked the biggest and loudest of the saloons and found the gambler studying the faro tables from the bar. Lassiter casually walked in and stood next to him.

"I don't recall inviting you to have a drink with me," the gambler turned and said.

"That's too bad," Lassiter said. "You're going to have to drink with me anyway."

The gambler started to turn from the bar, but Lassiter grabbed him by the collar. He quickly reached into the gambler's vest and pulled out the small Derringer pistol before the gambler had a chance to reach for it.

Lassiter shook his head. "This just isn't your day, is it, gambler? Let's take a walk."

The gambler walked out of the saloon in front of Lassiter, frequently turning back out of fear. Everyone was watching, noting the two black-handled .44s at Lassiter's side and the stern expression on his face. They were all commenting that the gambler had likely cheated the wrong man.

"Where are you taking me?" the gambler asked. "Do you intend to shoot me?"

"Just keep moving," Lassiter ordered. "If I would have wanted to kill you, I would have done it long before now."

"What do you want from me?" the gambler asked.

"Information," Lassiter said. They were standing

outside the saloon, and Lassiter had him backed up against the logs, bracing himself. "We can either go back in there and sit at a table, or we can talk out here."

"I have no intention of drinking with you," the gambler spat.

"Fine," Lassiter said. "Then we'll talk right here."

"No, I'm not talking with you at all," the gambler suddenly said, trying to push his way past Lassiter.

Again Lassiter grabbed him by the collar and slammed him back into the logs, knocking his hat off and the air from his lungs. The gambler slowly regained his breath with wide eyes.

"Let me go," the gambler demanded.

"If you start yelling," Lassiter warned, "I'm going to knock all your teeth out."

The gambler stood glaring at Lassiter. He had no choice but to stay where he was and let Lassiter talk. There were people starting to gather, but none of them interfered. They all knew about the gambler, and everyone was waiting for this to happen. The stage driver was among them, and he was already shaking his head, saying something about the tinhorn gambler not having the sense he was born with.

Lassiter was aware of the gathering crowd, but he had given the gambler a chance to talk in private. The gambler had not wanted to comply.

"I'm going to be brief," Lassiter said. "I don't want to ever see you on that stage again. And furthermore, I don't want to ever catch you in Glitter Creek. You got that?"

"You can't stop me from traveling," the gambler said.

"You just try me," Lassiter said. "And you might

be interested to know that Gil Driscoll is working with the Sloan Gang all the way. I don't know what he's told you, but you'd better not trust him.''

The gambler got a sudden look of guilt and then concern on his face, which quickly turned to anger.

"What are you talking about?" the gambler asked.

"You know what I'm talking about," Lassiter said. "I don't know what kind of deal you've got going with Driscoll, but people have seen you together over here. Maybe Big Jack Sloan would like to know about that."

"You're crazy," the gambler said.

"Well, maybe," Lassiter said, handing the Derringer back to the gambler. "But you're in a whole lot of trouble."

Lassiter turned and started to walk away from the gambler. He saw and heard the crowd gasp, and he knew the gambler was raising the Derringer. Lassiter wasn't surprised. In fact, he had expected it.

As the hammer on the gambler's Derringer clicked back, Lassiter spun in one motion, drew one of his black-handled .44s, and fired.

The gambler choked deep in his lungs as Lassiter fanned three bullets into his chest region. The Derringer fell to the ground without being fired, and the gambler pitched forward onto his face and lay still.

It was still for a time, and then the crowd began to rumble. The people started to gather around then, and the driver walked up to Lassiter, looking down at the gambler.

"I told you you should've made him walk," the driver said with a shake of his head. "He would've had a helluva lot better chance against Sloan and his bunch than he did against you."

* * *

The stage rolled back from Coeur d'Alene toward Glitter Creek, picking up a few passengers along the way. The trip was quiet, and nothing happened at all until a fly bit one of the horses in the team and nearly caused a runaway. But the driver got the team back together and the stage slowed, and everything went smooth down into town.

When the stage got into Glitter Creek, there was a whole contingent of armed men waiting for Lassiter. One of them even had Lassiter's sorrel stallion saddled and ready to go. Harold Mitchell and Lanna were both standing near the hotel, trying to talk over the shouting men.

Lassiter got the men to quiet down and Harold Mitchell stepped forward.

"They came into town and stole the doctor," Mitchell said. "It was in the middle of the night, and no one saw them do it. Now they have him up in the mountains at their hideout. He's the only doctor we've got."

"Let's go up and get him back!" one of the men yelled from his horse.

The others shouted in a chorus, and all the men were ready to ride out immediately. Lassiter got them quieted down again and told them all to think about something.

"How did they know where the doctor lived?" Lassiter asked them. "They couldn't come in here in the middle of the night and just locate the doctor just like that. Someone had to tell them where the doctor lived. Think about it. Who do you suppose told them?"

Everyone looked to one another, and they were all shrugging. Lassiter asked them if anyone had seen Gil Driscoll lately. Harold Mitchell spoke up immediately.

"He went over to Coeur d'Alene this morning," Mitchell said. "He told me he had to take care of some business. He seemed upset when he left."

Lassiter knew immediately that word about his killing the gambler had reached Glitter Creek before the stage. Driscoll could have left to avoid any confrontation, or he could be taking care of business. Either way, he still would have had plenty of time to tell the Sloan Gang where they could find the doctor.

But there was little use in trying to point out anything to anybody right now. The whole town was here, and they were angered about having their doctor abducted. No one had any doubts it had been the Sloan Gang who had taken him; news of the shootout during the attempted holdup had reached town within a matter of hours.

Now the main thing was to get the group of men settled down and made to understand a posse was a bad idea. They couldn't all ride down into Miner Canyon and expect to have anything more happen than to get shot up bad. Sloan and his gang would be expecting them. Even if Sloan was hurt, the others would fight to the end.

"What are we waitin' for?" one of the men spoke up. The others began to yell for Lassiter to lead them.

Lassiter got them quieted again and told them he wasn't going to lead them. When they had quit their groaning, he explained why.

"You don't go into an outlaw hideout on their terms," he said. "They'll be watching for somebody to be going down in there to get the doctor out. They'll just shoot everybody who goes in there."

"We've got way more men than they do," the man spoke up again. "We heard you killed two of them and shot old Sloan himself. Why don't we just finish them off?"

"We might get them finished off," Lassiter said. "But what if they decide to use the doctor as a hostage? What if they decide they just want to shoot him? Then we haven't accomplished anything. We've just succeeded in getting the doctor killed."

The men were rumbling again and Lassiter told them it would be best to take the gang by surprise when the time was right. There was nothing any of them could do at the present time to help the doctor. They would just have to wait and hope for the best.

After more discussion the men realized that Lassiter was right. They knew better than to think he was afraid to go over into Miner Canyon after the Sloan Gang; after what they had seen and heard about Lassiter, they realized he was just smart and knew how to stay alive. They knew that there was no doubt of the outcome when Lassiter got involved in a fight.

After the men were gone, Harold Mitchell asked Lassiter if he thought Gil Driscoll had had anything to do with the doctor being taken into Miner Canyon.

"You know what I think about Driscoll," Lassiter said, helping the driver unload baggage. "You don't have to ask me about the doctor."

"I've asked Gil Driscoll repeatedly if he is involved with Sloan," Mitchell said. "He is beginning to get angry with me. He has even talked about cutting off loan money."

"What do you need with loan money from him now anyway?" Lassiter asked. "With the amounts of gold you're getting from the mines, you should open your own bank."

Mitchell thought about it a moment. After a short

time he shrugged. "Gil has been a good friend to me. I can't see that he could be in with outlaws."

"Didn't you just say that he threw a temper tantrum and told you to be careful or he wouldn't loan you any more money?" Lassiter asked. "That sounds to me like he's really on the defensive."

"I still think you're wrong," Mitchell told Lassiter. "He can't be involved in all this. I've just got to see it to believe it."

Lassiter looked hard at him. "Sooner or later you will," he said. "If you're patient enough, and God knows you've been patient."

Harold Mitchell walked away and Lanna stayed behind. She watched Lassiter's frustration mount, and she asked him what he was going to do.

"I haven't got much choice but to just let things develop," Lassiter answered. "Driscoll is so slick that he manages to keep himself just a hair's breath ahead of everybody. He's never really there when things happen that he's caused. But someday he's going to make a mistake. And mark my word, I'm going to be there when that happens."

Suddenly there was yelling up the street, and a crowd gathered around a horse that was coming into town on its own. There was a body draped over its back and tied securely to the saddle. The man had been shot in the head.

Harold Mitchell came out of the hotel, and he walked over to Lassiter.

"That looks like the doctor," he said. "My God, what have they done to him?"

Lassiter and Harold Mitchell worked their way through the crowd to the horse. Lanna stayed back, unable to watch. Lassiter lifted the man's head and found that he had been shot in the face twice. It was the doctor, recognizable only by his clothes. And there was a note attached to his chest.

Lassiter read the words to the crowd: *He was not a very good doctor anyway.*

"Now what do you say about going after them?" the man who had spoken up earlier asked.

"There's still no use for anybody to get shot up," Lassiter said. "They'll be watching even closer for us now. This note says they weren't happy with the doctor, so they killed him. Maybe that means our troubles are over."

Everybody started talking again, wondering what had happened at the outlaw hideout to make them kill the doctor. The doctor had been exceptional in helping most people.

Then everyone quieted down once again as Lassiter said one last thing.

"The only reason I can see for them killing the doctor is that he couldn't save Sloan. Maybe Sloan is dead."

13

FOR THE NEXT COUPLE of weeks Lassiter fought the urge to lead a posse into Miner Canyon and get rid of the Sloan Gang once and for all. He knew now that Sloan was still alive and likely laying up in the cabin to heal his leg—as much as it would heal. He knew Sloan was still alive by the way Driscoll acted. Had Sloan been killed, Driscoll would be a lot more nervous than he was presently. The doctor had likely been killed so that he could never tell where the hideout was located.

As it was, Driscoll seemed to be getting more confident. He realized Harold Mitchell was behind him a hundred percent and that he didn't have to worry about anybody else. Mitchell carried the vast majority of the weight in town, and whatever suited Harold Mitchell was just fine with the town.

Lassiter realized that was good to a point. Mitchell was a fine and upstanding man, and he didn't use his power and influence to a negative degree, as Driscoll did. What Lassiter couldn't understand was why

Mitchell could not see through Driscoll for what he was. Lanna certainly had turned against Driscoll. But her father remained loyal to him.

It would seem so much simpler to just get rid of Sloan and his bunch. But Lassiter restrained himself, mainly because he knew Driscoll was keeping good track of what was going on in town and would certainly be able to get warning to Sloan ahead of time. In addition, the men of the town, especially the younger ones, were too eager and were hard to manage. That, combined with lack of experience, would mean a lot of dead young men once they got into Miner Canyon.

Lassiter knew that sooner or later Sloan would become impatient and want to make a move. That wouldn't occur this fall, though, Lassiter decided. Sloan's leg would have to mend, and he would have to get his gang built back up again. Both of those would take time, and when the following spring arrived, things would happen quickly.

As the summer ended and the leaves began to fall, Lassiter knew he had guessed correctly. The remaining stage runs went without incident. The town began to wind down for the winter, and Glitter Creek tried to forget, at least for the time being, that there was a gang of outlaws just waiting for the right opportunity to move in.

Lanna was keeping open company with Lassiter now. He didn't seem to mind, and her father had resigned himself to the fact that she was never going to be interested in Gil Driscoll. Lassiter was not going to be tied down, and Lanna had learned to respect that. What it did for both of them was to bring them together to work on the problem of getting her father to take a new course in Glitter Creek.

Lassiter took time each day to curry the sorrel stallion he now called his own, the one he had taken when the Sloan Gang had killed his own horse. The autumn days were now warm and bright, and Lassiter would take the stallion out along the creek. While he worked one afternoon to get the horse rubbed down, Lanna watched and reflected on the past summer in Glitter Creek.

"This town cannot stand another summer like the last one," she suddenly said. "People will stop coming here."

"You're right about that," Lassiter said.

"How do I go about getting my father to realize this, to see that he has to make some changes in his thinking?"

"We've talked about that before," Lassiter said. "Your father has to do his own changing. Nobody can do it for him."

"Lord knows we've pointed out the main problem here," Lanna said. "He has got to be able to see that Gil Driscoll is this town's biggest concern."

Lassiter stopped currying the horse for a moment. He was looking out over the mountains, where the high country was getting its first snowstorm.

"Maybe we can help your father see through Driscoll after all," Lassiter said.

"What do you mean?" Lanna asked.

Lassiter was still thinking. Finally he said, "Why don't you have your father tell Driscoll that he needs more money, to start a new bank."

"A new bank?" Lanna asked. "Why would my father want to start a new bank?"

"Because this town needs one," Lassiter said. "Certainly Driscoll won't want to go along with it. But have your father tell Driscoll he will have ownership in it as well, but that your father will run it himself. See what happens."

"Driscoll won't give him the money," Lanna said. "I'll be willing to bet on that."

"Let's hope he doesn't give your father the money," Lassiter said. "If he's smart, he will. But Driscoll is too greedy. He knows if your father started a bank of his own—even if he was half owner—most of the people would move their money to your father's bank."

"Do you suppose my father would even want to start a new bank?" Lanna asked.

"Convince him that he does," Lassiter said. "Soon those mines of his are going to be producing a lot of gold. He will need to start taking care of his own financial dealings, or find somebody he can trust. Driscoll thinks that when the Sloan Gang takes over the town, he will have control of the money. Show your father how much Driscoll is blinded by greed. Just see if Driscoll isn't unhappy about a new bank."

Lanna seemed to have gained some energy. She was now realizing that there was hope for Glitter Creek and her father sooner than she had expected.

"But what do we do about the Sloan Gang?" Lanna then asked.

"They will be coming sooner or later," Lassiter said. "And you may have to help with that as well."

"How can I help with that?" she asked.

Lassiter had finished currying the stallion, and he and Lanna began to walk back toward town.

"Remember how you took that rifle the first day, when I went to check on the stage after the road agents had robbed you all?" Lassiter asked.

Lanna nodded. That day, when she had been taken from the stage and hauled off on the road agent's horse, was one she would never forget the rest of her life. She remembered how Lassiter had handed her a rifle when he was going back over the hill. She had been ready to use it.

"I remember the day well," Lanna answered. "Are you saying I need to be able to use a rifle well?"

"That's what I'm saying," Lassiter answered with a nod. "Practice with that rifle. You never know when you'll need it."

Big Jack Sloan sat on his bunk, cleaning his rifle. He was finally able to get up and around for extended periods of time. But he would never get used to the fact that he was missing his left leg just above the knee.

Now his days and nights were filled with the obsession of killing Lassiter. His waking hours were spent visualizing how he would end the gunfighter's life—where it would happen and how. Sloan would smile to himself as he saw the picture in his mind: Lassiter falling from his guns, and Sloan shooting and shooting until Lassiter virtually disappeared in front of him.

But there were more pressing things to take care of before that happened, and Sloan knew he had to take each day at a time and prepare himself and the gang for the upcoming spring. Now that snow filled the mountain passes and valleys, there was little need to do anything but rest and let his leg mend—what there was left of it.

And there was the matter of Macey. Sloan was certain now that Macey intended to someday take over the gang for himself; he had that notion, in the back of his mind continuously. Sloan had spent time trying to understand why Macey had taken the pains to save him, to keep him alive. It seemed logical that Macey would have wanted him to die after Lassiter had shot him. But instead, Macey had gone to a lot of trouble to get a doctor into the hideout.

It was while he was cleaning his rifle and noticed the gleam of the metal barrel that he finally understood what was going on within Macey's mind. The gold— the nonexistent gold that he had told Macey was buried somewhere in the mountains. Macey was waiting to hear where that gold was.

Sloan remembered how he had told Macey that there was gold hidden somewhere so that Macey would be a more loyal member of the gang. He should have known at the time that Macey could never be loyal to anyone but himself. Now Macey wanted the gold for himself and the gang for himself. But that wasn't going to happen.

Sloan had already demoted Macey within the gang. Coleman had become Sloan's right-hand man. Coleman was eager to do what he was told, and he knew who the real boss of the gang was, while Macey was always trying to show everybody that he was smarter and made better decisions. There would be no more argument about what was to be done now that Coleman was carrying out orders.

Coleman had taken what was left of the gang back over into Montana Territory to recruit more men for the gang. This time they would leave Bannack alone and go instead to the saloons and dance halls of Butte and Helena. Those two towns were filled with the sort who wanted to make fast, easy money. And many of them had been road agents already at one time or another.

Meanwhile, Macey was out hunting elk for camp meat. He had been sent out alone and would likely be back before too much more time elapsed. He certainly hadn't been happy about the whole thing, but Sloan had told him to either go hunting like he was told, or ride on out of Miner Canyon and don't look back.

Sloan heard the sound of someone coming through the snow outside, and he pulled himself up onto his one good leg. He found the makeshift crutch he had fashioned out of a twisted pine tree and hobbled to the door.

Macey rode down from a trail in back of the cabin, dragging a quarter of an elk behind him. Sloan watched Macey riding slowly, looking around the country, no doubt thinking about what he was going to do now that he was just another member of the gang.

Sloan went back to the bunk and resumed cleaning the rifle. Macey came in the door and stomped the snow off his boots and warmed his hands over the cast-iron cookstove.

"Well, that's the last time I go hunting," he announced. "You can get one of the others to do it from now on."

Sloan continued to clean the rifle. He didn't bother to look up. "Wrong, Macey," he said. "You're going to be hunting meat for this outfit until I say different. And you're going to be cooking it until I say different. You might as well get used to that."

Macey stood near the stove, rubbing his hands together. His anger was rising steadily.

"What the hell is going on here?" he wanted to know. "Why are you picking on me like this?"

Now Sloan looked up. His eyes were narrowed. "Because you still don't know who runs this gang, that's why. You're just like some upstart kid in school who wants the teacher to think he knows more than she does. Kids like that either get booted out of school or wise up and pay attention. Which is it going to be for you?"

Macey stared at Sloan a moment, then turned back to look at his cold and blood-covered hands. As soon as they were warmed, he would wash the elk blood off them.

"When Lassiter shot you, I got you up out of that steep draw you rolled into and saved your life," Macey said. "Now you call me a school kid. A fine way to say thank you."

"That thank-you ain't the point here, Macey. You want control of this gang so bad you can taste it. That ain't going to happen. You'd better get that through your head."

Macey was silent again. From outside came the sounds of men on horses, a number of them. Coleman had returned from Montana with the new gang members. Macey was staring hard at the stove, and Sloan decided it was a good time to give him some more food for thought.

"There's one other thing, Macey," Sloan said. He waited for Macey to turn, while the men outside talked and laughed and got down from their horses. "There ain't no gold, Macey. No gold."

Macey got a startled expression on his face. "What did you say?"

"That's right. There's no gold buried anywhere. I just told you that to keep you in line. There's no gold."

Macey stared at him, as if he didn't want to believe it. How could there be no gold? Coleman came through the door with the others and they crowded Macey to get space near the stove. Sloan was loading his rifle and looking at Macey. Then Macey blinked and turned and went outside.

14

CHRISTMAS AND THE NEW YEAR were ushered in with much celebration, as Glitter Creek was looking ahead to its finest year ever. February brought warmth and melting snow, and a wider road was begun along the bottom, following the creek. It was felt by the townspeople that this would benefit Glitter Creek to a great degree.

The new road would make a more direct route to the first stage stop and would connect with the Mullen Road closer to the bottom of the mountains. This would bypass the treacherous part of the trail that led across the top and into the jaws of the Sloan Gang. At this time there was nothing more important than making Glitter Creek safe from them.

Lassiter helped fell trees and erect a log bridge across the creek in two places where the new road wound from one side to the other along the narrow valley. Nearly everyone in town helped, including Harold Mitchell. The only one not working on the road, and in fact openly distressed at the undertaking, was Gil Driscoll.

Lassiter was certain beyond any doubt now that Driscoll and Sloan had been collaborating on a plan to take over Glitter Creek as soon as possible. This new road was going to make robbing the stage a thing of the past. The new road cut a lot of miles off the old trail and would make it nearly impossible for the Sloan Gang to do their robbing and get back down into Miner Canyon quickly. Sloan was either going to have to move his hideout to just outside of town—not very likely—or take control of the stage business himself.

Sloan was definitely going to have to make his move in a short time, Lassiter knew, or the opportunity might be lost to him forever. Once the news of the new road got out, people would be coming in ever faster. Glitter Creek up to now had been a fairly remote place to get in to, but when the snow was gone for good, that would no longer be a reality.

Driscoll made a move that showed he was going to try and squeeze the town from his end. During one of the town meetings, he entered late and took the opportunity to announce to everyone that there would no longer be money available for loans, not until he decided for himself that the town was really going forward.

"Until you get rid of *that* man," he said, pointing at Lassiter, "I cannot consider that Glitter Creek is headed anywhere. He tells you all what to do, and it's not good for the town."

"What are you talking about?" Harold Mitchell asked.

"I don't want to discuss it any," Driscoll said.

"Then I'll tell everybody now how you already

turned me down,'' Mitchell said. "Both my daughter and Lassiter suggested I apply for more money from you to start a new bank. They said you would turn it down and that would prove that you are a part of the Sloan Gang. Does this mean that you are working with outlaws, Gil?''

"Nobody has been able to prove that I'm working with outlaws,'' Driscoll said. "And no one will ever be able to prove that. Now, unless you people listen to me and get rid of Lassiter, there will be no more money for this town.''

"Aren't you forgetting something?'' Lassiter asked Driscoll. "Don't you remember that Harold Mitchell has two active gold mines that are bringing in money? He could start his own bank easily. Then where would you be?''

Driscoll looked over to Harold Mitchell. "Do you know anything about banking, Harold?'' he asked.

"I believe I could learn,'' Mitchell answered. "I believe I could learn pretty fast, as a matter of fact.''

"That's not a good idea,'' Driscoll said. "Good day, gentlemen.''

Driscoll then turned and walked out of the meeting without another word. Everyone broke into a clamor, and Harold Mitchell finally got them quieted down.

"Not long back Mr. Lassiter here asked me if I would consider starting a new bank,'' Mitchell told the others. "At the time I thought the idea ludicrous. Now I'm not so sure.''

The others broke into discussion again. Everyone was mad at Driscoll, and now they could all see that Lassiter had likely been right all along. Driscoll was probably working with the Sloan Gang, and he wanted

Lassiter gone so he could more easily help take the town over.

"We're behind you one hundred percent if you want to start a new bank," one of the businessmen said. "I say let's get to building it as soon as the new road is finished."

There were a lot of voices agreeing, and it was decided that as soon as the new road along the bottom was completed, lumber would be cut and brought along this road to begin construction of the new bank. Nobody seemed too worried about how to run the bank; they would learn that soon enough. And they wouldn't have to follow Driscoll's instructions.

Harold Mitchell suggested that the bank be jointly owned by the businessmen of the community and run the same way as the town council made decisions about Glitter Creek. A board of directors would be elected, and since everyone in town had the same interests, there would be little to discuss but getting the bank running. The idea passed and the men most interested in investing in the new bank met after the main meeting was adjourned.

Lassiter made his way back over to the hotel and joined Lanna for an evening meal. As usual, she was dressed in a fashionable gown and had her red hair piled up in curls under a silk hat.

"I think this town is going to move forward pretty fast now," Lassiter said. "Your father has decided to open another bank."

Lanna clapped for glee. "What made him finally come to his senses?" she asked.

"Gil Driscoll walked in and announced that he was cutting off all loans," Lassiter said with a laugh. "I guess Driscoll isn't as smart as I thought he was. He wants me out of town, and he thought his little threat was going to turn everyone against me. Your father spoke up in my behalf and said he wanted to open a bank in competition with Driscoll. That made everyone happy.''

''I can't see that anything but good can come of all this,'' Lanna said.

''Good will be the eventual outcome,'' Lassiter agreed. ''But there'll be hell to pay here soon.''

''What do you mean?'' Lanna asked.

''Driscoll will get word of this to Sloan. Then Sloan and his bunch will come down here as soon as they can and start the process of taking over the town.''

''How soon do you suppose this will happen?'' Lanna asked, concern in her voice.

''To tell you the truth,'' Lassiter answered, ''I can't understand why they haven't already made their move. Sloan must be getting organized. But sooner or later things are going to get hot in Glitter Creek.''

Sloan didn't think his gang was ready to hit Glitter Creek just yet. Coleman had chosen six good men to join the others, but they were all still getting used to one another. From experience Sloan knew that a group of road agents worked best when they all knew one another well.

The gang was now back up to good strength again—even better than when Lassiter had shot them up the first time while they had been robbing the stage. Counting Sloan, the gang now numbered a baker's dozen. There seemed to be little internal conflict between the new men and the other gang members from before, except that the problem of Macey still existed.

He was remaining with the gang, even though Sloan

had told him there was no gold. Besides, no one else paid him much attention anymore. They all knew Coleman was second in line. No one was going to question that. But Sloan was just waiting for Macey to get the idea he wasn't needed.

Macey had become even more sullen since the day when he had brought in the hind quarter of elk and Sloan had told him there was no gold. Macey still didn't know whether to think that was true or not, but he was sticking around for some reason.

But no one seemed to acknowledge he was even there. The weather was breaking now, and the ice and snow were melting from the streams. The other men went out for short rides, and Macey remained off by himself.

Then finally he approached Sloan and wanted to know if there really wasn't any gold buried anywhere.

"I told you there wasn't," Sloan growled. "No use asking again."

That seemed to settle things for Macey. Over the next few days he spent his time collecting his things and piling them in one corner. Finally Macey caught his horse while the others went down to the creek to wash clothes. When he was saddled and ready to pack his belongings, he came to Sloan.

"I'm pulling out," he told Sloan.

Sloan looked at him without surprise. "I figured you would sooner or later," Sloan said. "I guess you just don't fit in anymore."

"It used to be good here," Macey said, loading his belongings into his saddlebags. "But you had to go down into Bannack, even though I didn't think it was a good idea, and you had to bring Coleman into the gang. Now he's your main man and I'm out."

"You brought it on yourself, Macey."

"Yeah, well, I'm not so sure that your little group is ever going to get Glitter Creek," Macey said. "You've got to get through that gunfighter, Lassiter, and there's nobody here that can match him. I was the closest."

Sloan laughed. "You think you were ever a match for Lassiter?"

"Closer than anybody here," Macey said. "And that includes you."

Sloan was quiet for a moment. "Maybe before the son of a bitch shot me I could have beat him. Now it will be harder."

"Well, that's just it," Macey said, pulling himself up into the saddle. "You probably never could have taken him. But there's no way anymore, not since you're just half a man."

Macey turned and rode away from the cabin while Sloan glared after him. He yelled at Macey and told him to come back. He told Macey he would fight him man to man, and then they would see who was half a man. The other men down at the creek turned to see what was happening. But Macey was gone and all they could see was Sloan hobbling on his crutch, with one fist in the air.

In the days that followed, Sloan took the time to learn to ride with just one good leg. It was frustrating, but he was determined to get it done. He had to swing himself up from the horse's right side, instead of the usual left, and he had to remember that he didn't have the balance in the saddle that he had once had.

In addition Sloan had to learn how to carry his crutch while riding and at the same time pull his rifle when he needed it. It was a lot of work getting himself used to the changes, but he wasn't going to give up, no matter what.

For Sloan it was the most awkward experience of his life. However difficult it had been for him to live through the leg amputation, there were times when he wished he hadn't let Macey save him. Now he was never going to be what he once was, and all the men could see that. Some of them even felt sorry for him and that made him all the madder.

His hatred for Lassiter grew deeper and deeper. Sloan never quit his working to get ready for the day when he would again meet Lassiter and settle the score. He continued to spend hours getting used to riding, so that when the right time came he could stay on his horse. He was going to get Lassiter if it was the last thing he ever did.

Late one evening Coleman and two of the others came in from hunting to tell Sloan they had found fresh horse tracks up above the cabin. They had also found a place where somebody had been camping recently. Coleman was smiling as he talked about it, for he had found a glove the man had lost. It was one of Macey's.

"I should have known," Sloan said. "Macey is up there watching us."

"Shall we go after him?" Coleman asked.

"Let me handle this," Sloan said. "This has been coming for a long time."

15

EARLY THE NEXT MORNING Sloan took a shovel from one corner of the cabin and some old sacks they were using to get the fires started in the stove. With his makeshift crutch, Sloan hobbled out the door to his horse. Coleman was beside him, holding the horse and the shovel while Sloan got into the saddle. Then Coleman handed him the shovel.

"What are you going to do with that shovel?" Coleman asked.

"Dig a grave," Sloan said.

"Macey's?"

"Who else?"

"What if he gets you?" Coleman asked.

"Then you boys can cut cards for my horse," Sloan said with a thin smile. "But look for me to be back before suppertime."

"You sure you don't want somebody to come along?" Coleman asked.

"It's got to be me," Sloan answered. "I need to do

this myself, anyway—to prove I can kill a man who needs killing, even though I don't have a leg.''

Sloan rode out from the cabin and up the side of the mountain. The sun was just above the top of the peaks, and the day was open and bright. Sloan got halfway up the mountain when he realized someone was watching him. He rode on, confident that his plan was going to work.

After a few more miles of riding, Sloan worked his horse down through a patch of thick timber to the edge of a creek. He got down from his horse and moved into a growth of willows along the shoreline, taking the shovel and the rifle in with him. Once deep in the willows he could look out, while no one else could look in.

It was a perfect setup. Sloan began to dig and make noise in the willows, looking out on occasion to see if he couldn't spot Macey somewhere in the timber. After a short while he did see Macey, crouched nearby with a Winchester.

Sloan continued to make noise in the willows. Close to the creek he picked up some rocks and filled the two bags, then rubbed them with dirt and mud to make it look like he had just taken them out of the ground.

Sloan hobbled out from the willows with the two bags of rocks and dropped them to the ground. Then he turned and went back into the willows and began to dig again, as if getting more gold from the hole.

After digging for a time longer, Sloan moved himself over a ways through the willows and peered out from a different angle. He could see Macey at the edge of the thick patch of timber. Macey was watching the bags, thinking they were gold, and Sloan could almost see his mouth salivating.

Sloan brought his Winchester up and slowly cocked the hammer back. He told himself not to be anxious, to wait until he got a better shot at Macey. But he worried that Macey would not move and would soon become suspicious if there weren't any more sounds of digging coming from the willows. He knew he had to shoot soon, whether it was a good shot or not.

There was other movement off to Macey's right, and Sloan turned to see a small herd of elk moving through the timber to water. But they had spotted Macey and were walking slowly through the timber, trying to understand what he was. The wind was such that they couldn't smell either Macey or Sloan, and they were confused.

Macey saw the elk and looked for a time. Then he turned his attention back to the sacks that he thought were gold, resting just beside the willows.

Then Sloan held his breath. Macey was moving through the thick patch of timber down toward the willows. He had his own rifle ready and was still staring at the two sacks of rocks near the willows. He moved very slowly along the edge of the timber and then out into the open. Then he stopped to check his rifle.

Sloan took the opportunity and raised his Winchester. The shot cracked out from the willows and echoed through the surrounding forest. The bullet took Macey in the stomach, doubling him over into a writhing ball on the ground. Sloan laughed and came out of the willows.

He stuck his crutch under his arm and hobbled up to Macey, who was groaning in pain. Sloan was still laughing.

"Don't you remember, Macey? I told you there was

no gold. Them bags got rocks in them is all.'' He laughed again.

Sloan turned around as the herd of elk broke out of the timber just at the edge of the creek. They had heard the shot but were still confused. While he was turned, Macey fought the pain and grabbed his rifle. He grunted and raised the barrel. He fired just as Sloan turned back around.

The blast and Macey's movement scared the elk into a dead run across the creek. Sloan yelled and fell flat on his face. The bullet had entered his good leg, halfway up the shin, splintering the bones into fragments.

Sloan was still yelling when Coleman and four others of the gang came down the trail. Macey was trying to lever another round into his own rifle, but was nearly passed out from the pain in his stomach.

Coleman quickly saw what was happening and jumped down from his horse. Macey was trying to turn on his knees to aim at Coleman. But Coleman pulled his revolver and shot into Macey's face, blowing out the back of his head. Macey dropped the rifle and fell immediately forward onto his stomach.

Coleman then turned to Sloan, who was writhing on the ground from his leg wound. One of the outlaws moved away from Macey's body and took out a whiskey bottle.

"Pour that down him. Then we'll tie him on his horse and get him back to the cabin.''

"That leg don't look good,'' another one of the outlaws said.

"He'll have to make it on his own,'' Coleman said, lifting Sloan's head to pour whiskey down him. "We ain't going after any more doctors.''

* * *

Sloan spent another month in bed. One of the outlaws brought from Butte had been an army surgeon for the Confederacy. His name was Morrison, and he had managed to save Sloan's other leg with a combination of whiskey and a pair of tweezers, with which he picked bone fragments for three hours after the shooting. The leg was mending, but part of the feeling was gone.

Now Sloan worried about how he was going to oversee the spring activity. His leg was going to heal, but it wasn't going to be the same as it was, and he wasn't going to be able to get around very well at all. Realizing this, he knew that he was going to have to become twice as tough on everybody as he had been before.

Sloan quickly began to wonder if he could continue to lead the gang. No one paid much attention to him now, and the continuous stress and lack of self-confidence were beginning to turn his mind into funny shapes. He had dreams about being flat on the ground and unable to move, while the gang rode their horses over the top of him. All he could see were the underbellies of the horses and their hooves narrowly missing his face.

Finally Sloan resigned himself to the fact that he was going to have to use Coleman to help him with getting things started. Sloan had moved his meeting place with Driscoll from the pass to a heavy grove of quaking aspens farther down along the mountain. When there was a scheduled meeting with Driscoll, he sent Coleman and told him to make sure he heard what was going on down below.

Coleman gladly accepted the responsibility and

learned a number of things from Driscoll that he did not share with Sloan. Coleman decided that sooner or later everyone was going to be tired of having a cripple for a leader and that he would necessarily take over then. The less Sloan knew about what was going on, the better.

While Sloan remained inactive, Coleman took it upon himself to make periodic trips down into Glitter Creek and make contact with Driscoll. He never told Sloan or any of the others, thinking it was best to keep it from them until the time was right. Besides, he liked Glitter Creek. No one knew him there, and that made it easy to come and go without creating a disturbance. He was careful not to create alarm or to ride blatantly in front of the gunfighter, Lassiter, who was working with most of the townspeople building a new road out of town.

Coleman learned from Driscoll that they were building the road through the lower part of the draw where the creek moved out into the main valley. This would help them save time during their stage runs and keep them away from the road agents that rode the higher mountain trails. Coleman knew this meant they would have to act fast in order to take over the town.

"This don't look good to us," Coleman was telling Driscoll late one evening in Driscoll's office.

"Of course it doesn't," Driscoll said. "It means the stage will be bypassing the roughest part of the road, where the stage was easy to hold up. I would say the easiest thing to do is move right now against the town. How is Sloan doing?"

Coleman shrugged. "I don't know if he can remain in charge much longer. He's just now getting so he can walk slowly. It's hard to say when he'll be able to ride, or even if he'll ever be able to ride again.''

"They're going to be done with that road before too much longer," Driscoll said. "We can't wait for Sloan to move against this town.''

"What's the big hurry?" Coleman wanted to know. "I realize you and Sloan have wanted to move fast, but I haven't understood why yet.''

"That's simple," Driscoll said. "As soon as that road is complete, they're going to be moving lumber into town to start a new bank. That means everyone will be drawing their money out of this bank. And you know what kind of problem that will be.''

"You can stall them off," Coleman said. "You can tell them they can't have their money right away.''

"You come in here and tell them they can't have their money," Driscoll challenged. "You don't have to face those people. They're already suspicious of me. I'm not going to make them sure about things.''

"I can see you have a problem," Coleman said. "But I can't do anything until Sloan gets better.''

Driscoll was getting angry now, and he was ready to raise his voice. But he didn't want to draw any undue attention to himself and Coleman from the employees and patrons of the bank.

"Now, you listen," Driscoll said, gritting his teeth. "Sloan promised me he would see to it that the gang was ready to take this town just as soon as I had things lined up down here. I've done my share, and I expect some cooperation from your end.''

Coleman shrugged again. "I'll tell Sloan you've got ants in your pants. But I can't promise anything.''

Driscoll began to drum his fingers against the table. "I'll tell you what," he finally said. "You go back up and tell Sloan that I'm about to change sides in this thing. I might just as well go along with the townspeople now and just let Lassiter know that Sloan is shot up. Then he can lead some men up there, and I'll be a hero.''

Coleman grunted. "We've got a lot of new men. He would be crazy to lead a bunch of raw miners and businessmen into Miner Canyon after us. That's why he hasn't done it before."

"Just think of it this way," Driscoll said. "I've spent a lot of time getting things put together down here. I don't want to have wasted all that time. If that new bank goes up and everybody wants to switch their money over, then I've wasted my time. One way or another I'm going to win in this thing."

Coleman thought a moment about what Driscoll had said. It made sense. He had done a good job of getting everything organized from his position for a smooth takeover of the town. But due to circumstances beyond his control, his efforts were going to be for nothing before long.

Coleman decided it wouldn't be a bad idea to keep this man on their side.

"I'll tell you what," Coleman finally told Driscoll. "You keep working down here, and I'll see to it that you don't lose out. We'll watch for the lumber that's coming, and when the time comes, we'll get Glitter Creek. Big Jack Sloan or no Big Jack Sloan, we'll get Glitter Creek."

16

THE ROAD WAS COMPLETED the last day of April, and
the town held a celebration, even though a late snowstorm came in and dumped a foot of wet snow and
turned the streets into a mud pit. All the business-
people took the day off, and everyone went to the
hotel to celebrate.

The first stage run of the spring was set for the next
day along the new road. Harold Mitchell and the other
businessmen seemed to have forgotten about the Sloan
Gang for the most part. It had been some time since
anything had happened and everyone was content to
think Sloan had left the country.

Now that the road was completed, there was already
a freight wagon in town and more on the way. This
included a number of wagons that were to come in
later in the day, loaded with lumber for the new bank.
Everyone was looking forward to getting the construction started.

Lassiter wasn't sure how much Driscoll knew about
the new bank and how soon it would be up and ready

to take his business away from him. If Driscoll knew anything at all, Lassiter had the feeling that things would be happening soon. Driscoll wasn't one to roll over and play dead.

But Driscoll had been staying pretty close to town, and this had Lassiter wondering. It could only mean that he was meeting somebody in town on occasion, somebody nobody recognized. Lassiter was sure he hadn't seen anyone unusual; but he had been working with the others building the road and wasn't able to see everyone that came and went.

Since nothing had been happening, Harold Mitchell and the other businessmen seemed content to think things would go smoothly from here on out. So the reason to celebrate seemed appropriate in everyone's mind. But Lassiter was not so sure.

While the townspeople had a good time, Lassiter sat in the window, reading a paper that had come over from Coeur d'Alene. He looked up when when he heard Lanna calling him. She was standing near the door, looking out into the street. Lassiter got up and looked to where she was pointing.

Two men were tying their horses in front of the bank. Neither Lanna nor Lassiter recognized either one of them. One was tall and thin and dark-featured. He carried himself like he wasn't concerned about who saw him or what they thought of him.

Both men went into the bank, and Lassiter now realized that Driscoll had been seeing someone in town all this time. He turned to Lanna.

"What will you bet they're part of Sloan's bunch?" he said.

"What are they doing riding in here as bold as you please?" Lanna asked. "Why would they do that?"

"Something big is happening," Lassiter said. "Otherwise they wouldn't be riding in here like that. Those two have information of some kind for Driscoll, and they want to tell him in a hurry. I think I'll go over and join in."

Lanna took his arm. "Lassiter, what if they try to kill you?"

"Wouldn't be the first time that's happened," Lassiter answered.

He left Lanna with a worried look on her face and started over toward the bank. The snow had melted for the most part, and the streets were muddy. People were coming and going, but Lassiter kept his eyes on the bank.

As Lassiter walked through the front door, he noticed the two strangers in Driscoll's office. Driscoll's eyes got big, but before he could send the two men out, Lassiter was inside the office.

"Thought I'd sit in," Lassiter said. "I like to know what's happening in the banks these days."

Driscoll suddenly got confident. He noticed the two men with him watching Lassiter, looking him up and down and noticing his black attire and the two pistols at his side. Yet neither of them was afraid of Lassiter. In fact, Coleman in particular had an arrogant attitude. He was glaring at Lassiter.

That was good, Driscoll thought. He cleared his throat and sat back in his chair.

"Lassiter, this is Mr. Coleman and Mr. Morrison. They've come to make a deposit."

Lassiter nodded. "They both look like upstanding citizens to me. Now that their deposit is made, it's time for them to be riding on."

Driscoll looked at the two outlaws. "I don't think

Mr. Coleman or Mr. Morrison is ready to leave yet, are you, gentlemen?"

"You're both ready to leave, aren't you?" Lassiter said. "I have a deposit to make myself. And Mr. Driscoll needs my undivided attention."

Coleman continued to glare, and Morrison began to loosen his fingers on his gun hand. Lassiter spread his legs ever so slightly and relaxed his arms at his sides.

Driscoll suddenly became alarmed and stood up. "Listen," he said to Coleman and Morrison, "why don't you two wait out back for just a few minutes while I talk with Mr. Lassiter. It will be just a minute, and I will send him out to get you when he's through here." He winked at the two of them.

Coleman and Morrison both nodded. They turned and walked past Lassiter out the back door. Lassiter looked at Driscoll a moment and began to smile.

"That's nice, Driscoll," he said. "But I didn't say they could come back. I'll go tell them that right now."

"Where do you think you're going so fast?" Driscoll asked.

"I told you," Lassiter said. "To send your two friends out of town. I know they're both waiting to greet me out back."

Lassiter walked slowly out of Driscoll's office and held up just before he went through the back door. He noticed it was slightly ajar, and through the crack he could see that Morrison was waiting for him behind the door, his hand raised with his gun in it.

Rather than have a gun slammed into his head, Lassiter decided to reverse the outcome. With all his might he rammed the door back and into Morrison, crushing him up against the side of the bank.

Morrison groaned and his gun dropped to the ground. Lassiter then slammed his fist into Morrison's face, and he bounced off the wall once again and fell face forward into the mud. Lassiter then heard the hammer of a revolver click just behind him.

"You made a mistake, Lassiter. Now you're dead."

Lassiter turned to see Coleman aiming his pistol at him. Coleman was sneering and Lassiter could tell he loved to kill. But before he could pull the trigger, there came a voice from just to his right.

"Drop that gun or I'll shoot you!"

Lanna was standing nearby with her rifle aimed at Coleman. The outlaw turned slightly to look at her and backed up, keeping his gun on Lassiter.

"No, lady," he said, "I'm aimin' to shoot this Lassiter fellow. You understand."

"I said drop the gun," Lanna repeated.

"Shoot him, Lanna," Lassiter said. "He hasn't got the guts to use that gun."

Coleman turned to look at Lassiter. He couldn't believe what Lassiter had just said. Lanna then raised her rifle to her shoulder.

"Go ahead and shoot," Lassiter said. He was holding his hands next to his twin .44s, one on each hip.

Coleman weighed the odds. He knew that Lassiter would draw just as soon as he made a move to shoot. And even if he got Lassiter, the woman would kill him.

"Wait!" Coleman suddenly said. "Just hold on now. Maybe we can talk."

"Drop the gun," Lanna said.

"She's not going to say it again," Lassiter warned.

Coleman dropped his pistol and stepped back with his hands held up. Lassiter reached down and picked up the pistol. From just behind Lassiter there came movement, and Lanna turned her rifle and fired.

The bullet whined off the pistol Morrison had dropped when Lassiter had crushed him with the door. Morrison had been jumping to get it, and Lanna had seen him in time. Now he pulled his hand back and stared at Lanna. He couldn't believe how well she could shoot.

"You're lucky she didn't want to kill you," Lassiter said.

Coleman still had his hands raised, and he was backing up farther now.

"What are you going to do with us?" he asked.

"Get on your horses, both of you, and tell Sloan to get out of the country," Lassiter said. "This banker, Driscoll, is through here. His bank is closing. Sloan and the rest of you have no chance to take over Glitter Creek now. It's time you all moved out."

Coleman was shaking his head. "Big Jack Sloan ain't about to move out on your say-so, even if you shot one of his legs off. He's comin' down here after you."

"Good," Lassiter said. "Tell him to come soon, or I'm going up after him."

Coleman and Morrison got on their horses and rode out as fast as they could. Lassiter looked to Lanna and thanked her for saving his life.

"You did that for me once," she said. "Turnabout is fair play."

"Let's go talk to Driscoll," Lassiter said.

"I'm with you," Lanna said with a nod.

Lassiter and Lanna both stormed through the back door and went straight to Driscoll's office. It was closed and locked; without hesitation, Lassiter began pounding on it.

"It's time we had a serious talk!" Lassiter yelled through the door.

"I'm not talking to you," Driscoll answered. "Now go away!"

Lanna was beside Lassiter now. She was as angry as he, and she meant to talk to Driscoll.

"This is Lanna Mitchell!" she yelled through the door. "I need to talk to you!"

"You're just fronting for Lassiter!" Driscoll yelled back. "I won't open the door."

"If you open it for me, I will talk to you alone," Lanna said. "Lassiter will stay out here. I can talk to you alone."

"The answer is still no," Driscoll said.

Lanna backed away from the door and looked at Lassiter. He seemed calm, as usual, but there was a glint in his eye.

"Step back just a little more, Lanna, if you please," Lassiter said. "I'm going to rearrange Driscoll's door for him."

With a terrific smash from his boot, Lassiter slammed the door inward, knocking off two hinges and leaving the door hanging awkwardly from its frame.

"I said we needed to talk, Driscoll," Lassiter said. "And that's just what we're going to do."

17

LASSITER STOOD IN FRONT of Driscoll's desk, his hands at his sides. He was watching Driscoll, who moved nervously behind his desk. Lanna pointed out that Driscoll had his hand near one of the desk drawers.

Lassiter nodded. "I can see that. I'm just waiting for him to bring a gun up so I'll have an excuse to put him out of his misery forever."

Driscoll sat back in his chair with a look of defeat.

"I'll bet that was some of Sloan's men who just left," Lassiter said. "I know they were friends of yours."

"No friends of mine," Driscoll said.

Lassiter stood over Driscoll's desk and put his hands down on the top and leaned over. Driscoll recoiled.

"I think you had better take your little banking enterprise elsewhere," Lassiter suggested. "Because by this time next month, there is going to be a new bank in town."

Driscoll said nothing. He just stared at Lassiter.

"You haven't been at the town council meetings lately," Lassiter said. "We told you at the last meeting you attended that Lanna's father would likely open a bank in competition with you. Now that is going to happen for sure. All your customers will be gone from here in less than a month."

"Is that so?" Driscoll said.

Lassiter pointed out the window to where a caravan of wagons was just pulling into town. There were six in all, and they were laden with fresh lumber.

"Those wagons will unload today, and that lumber will be a new bank in no time at all."

"Lassiter's right," Lanna said to Driscoll. "My father has finally come to his senses. He's starting his own bank. That way he can take better care of his money."

Driscoll didn't bother to acknowledge that Lanna had spoken. He was still staring at Lassiter. Outside, the wagons were rolling past with the lumber, and people were coming from the celebration in the hotel to gather in the streets and cheer. Driscoll didn't even bother to look.

"I've known about this little plan all along," Driscoll said haughtily. "Is that what you broke my door down to tell me?"

"What do you mean, you've known about it?" Lanna said.

"I've known about it," Driscoll repeated. "Now, is there more that you have to tell me?"

"There's more," Lassiter said. "You might want to listen."

"Well, please hurry," Driscoll said. "I have an appointment."

"The townspeople are pulling their money out of here," Lassiter said. "And you had better hope it's all here for them when they come after it."

"They'll get all that's coming to them," Driscoll said. He was sneering.

"When they've gotten their money," Lassiter then said, "it might be wise if you decided to move. I've given Coleman and Morrison an eviction notice for Sloan. I'm giving you one right now."

Driscoll grunted and got up from his chair. He pushed past Lassiter and Lanna to get to his hat. Then he huffed through the broken-down door and out of the bank. He stood on the boardwalk for a time longer and watched men unloading the lumber across the street. Finally he turned and walked away toward his little house at the edge of town.

"How do you suppose he knew about the lumber that was coming in?" Lanna asked.

"Coleman and Morrison likely told him," Lassiter said. "They came in here with a message from Sloan, just as sure as the sun is shining. I should have known."

"You look worried now," Lanna said. "What's the matter?"

"I wish I could get someone to guard that stage tomorrow instead of me," Lassiter said. "I have a feeling Driscoll is going to be working with Sloan and Coleman to try and get rid of the competition."

"Driscoll is certainly mad, isn't he?" Lanna said.

Lassiter nodded. "You had better talk your father into having a lot of men guarding those workers tomorrow when they get started building the bank. I

157

think Driscoll and Sloan already have something planned."

Lassiter sat having coffee with the stage driver while the blacksmith worked to get the rim back on the repaired wheel. A cracked spoke had been discovered just before the stage was to leave, and now all the passengers were grumbling about the delay. Lassiter reminded them how much more time they would have lost had the wheel broken down out in the middle of the mountains, where there was no blacksmith.

Lanna was over with her father, watching the beginning construction that was taking place on the new bank. Everyone in town seemed happy that things were again progressing. Spring had come and more people were coming into Glitter Creek. It promised to be the best year ever.

Lassiter had been watching for Driscoll ever since the wheel had been taken off the stage for repair. Driscoll usually kept a close watch on who came and went on the stage. But this morning he was nowhere to be seen, and it made Lassiter suspicious.

After considerable thought, Lassiter walked down to where the bank was being built. Everyone was in good spirits, and the work was going quickly. Lassiter found Harold Mitchell and Lanna standing together, talking about the future.

"Why don't we postpone the first stage run until tomorrow?" Lassiter asked. "I don't have a good feeling about today."

"We can't do that," Harold Mitchell said. "There are a lot of people who are traveling. We can't keep them here."

"I don't see Driscoll anywhere," Lassiter pointed out. "That also makes me nervous."

"Maybe he took your advice and moved out," Mitchell said.

"Not likely," Lassiter said.

"We have to get the stage over to Coeur d'Alene," Mitchell told Lassiter. "The weather has opened up, and this town is popping at the seams."

Lassiter looked around. "Have you got enough men here watching things with you? I only see a couple."

"I'll have more shortly," Mitchell said. "Some of the men are doing morning chores. They should be in soon."

Lassiter nodded. "Well, I'll get the stage rolling."

The passengers boarded the stage, eager to get moving. They were all excited about being the first to ride the stage over the new road. But Lassiter didn't share in their enthusiasm. He tied his sorrel stallion on behind the stage, just in case he needed to get back to town in a hurry.

Lassiter climbed up with the driver. People had gathered to see the stage off, and they were all cheering. Lassiter began to think he was overreacting and possibly worrying about nothing. He and the driver talked while the driver spit his tobacco and started the team ahead. They were leaving town, and no one seemed concerned about the least little thing.

The day was open and bright, and the birds were singing in the trees along the creek. A woman and her family riding into town in a buggy waved as they passed on the road. Lassiter finally allowed himself to relax. He hoped everyone was right about being free of worries now in Glitter Creek.

*　　*　　*

Big Jack Sloan got up from the bed and found his crutch. He fought the pain in his leg and hobbled outside to get his horse. He met Gil Driscoll, who was watching the other men catch their horses in the corral.

"You're sure that Lassiter left with the stage?" Sloan asked Driscoll again. He had been quizzing him all morning, ever since he had arrived from town to bring the news.

Driscoll nodded. "I'm sure they were leaving today. I saw them getting the stage hitched up early this morning."

Sloan nodded. "You stay here till we get back. Got that?"

"You've told me that about six times, Jack."

"Well, I'm telling you again. Don't go anywhere till we get back here from town. You got it?"

Driscoll nodded again. "Sure, Jack. Anything else?"

"Just be here when we get back, Driscoll. And change your attitude."

Driscoll turned away from Sloan so that Sloan wouldn't see his thin little smile. Sloan was already suspicious that Driscoll and Coleman had been meeting for some time and that the information they were sharing was something he wasn't getting in on. But today he intended to change everything. Sloan realized that it was all on the line now.

Morrison, the ex-Confederate who had been a surgeon, walked over to Sloan. He was leading his horse and holding on to his saddle.

"I would stay here if I was you," Morrison told Sloan. "I seen legs like that in the war. They get bad when you walk on them before they're healed."

"The leg ain't that bad," Sloan argued.

"Why don't you let Coleman lead us down into Glitter Creek?" Morrison asked. "You could stay up here and get better and take over the next time."

"I said no!" Sloan was so mad he could hardly keep himself still. He was weaving on the crutch, biting his lip against the pain. "I said I was leading this raid. Now, everyone saddle up!"

The rest of the gang, including Coleman, was standing around listening. They all realized that Sloan wasn't able to lead them down. There was little choice now but to do what he told them. It was either that or somebody kill him. And no one seemed ready to do that yet.

They all rode behind Sloan, their progress slowed by the fact that Sloan could not hold himself in the saddle very well at all. But he was not going to admit to anyone that things were going downhill for him at a rapid rate.

Sloan managed to take his mind off the pain by chewing on small pieces of pine he stuck into his mouth. There was a job to get done now, pain or no pain, and it was important that he lead them through this.

In time they reached the slopes above Glitter Creek. They could see all the activity in town, and it seemed that everyone was content and happy—nobody really expecting anything to happen.

Big Jack Sloan led the way down the slope. Coleman was right behind him, and the others in the gang followed. They stayed deep in the trees to avoid being detected as they watched the men working down below on the new bank building. Sloan smiled to himself:

Soon that new bank building was going to be nothing but charred rubble.

The excitement built in Sloan, and he forgot about his injured leg. He laughed and kicked his horse into a dead run out of the trees and down the slope. Coleman and the others followed close behind, their guns raised. They began to yell and whoop and shoot their guns off, as if they were headed to a carnival.

As they neared the town, Sloan could see the people scattering from the street like so many terrified chickens. They could see the workers at the new bank dropping their tools to run for cover. There were a number of men who were guarding the bank, and they were now scurrying to pick up their rifles. They had become lax and had laid them aside.

Once in town, Sloan and his gang began to run people down. Some were shot and left for dead, while others were merely run down with horses and injured. Coleman delighted in killing most of those he ran down. Even those who went into buildings and shops for cover were shot at, as Sloan and the others riddled everything with bullets.

Sloan now wished Lassiter were here so he could kill the man. He wanted desperately to have a chance at Lassiter once again. Harold Mitchell had hired Lassiter, and Sloan could see Mitchell working to get a rifle ready to fire. Sloan decided today was a good day to get revenge for what Lassiter had done to his leg.

Sloan rode his horse toward Mitchell, yelling as he went. Mitchell saw him and tried to duck underneath a wagon. But he was too slow, and Sloan shot at him with his pistol. He saw Harold Mitchell's head snap back and saw him fall downward into the wheel of the wagon.

Sloan laughed as he saw Harold Mitchell fall. He turned his horse toward the new bank, which was starting to erupt into flames. Coleman and two others had set it afire. Sloan was happy now; he was soon going to own Glitter Creek.

18

SLOAN TURNED ON HIS HORSE to take another look at the flames, but suddenly saw that he was a target himself. Lanna Mitchell was running toward him with a Winchester. She acted as if she knew how to use the rifle.

Coleman and Morrison had almost been killed by her when visiting Driscoll at the bank, and Sloan had found out about the incident. Sloan knew from what Coleman and Morrison had said about her that she was a good shot. He quickly turned his horse and rode among some of his men.

Sloan turned and could see her firing her rifle, dropping the men in front of him to get her sights on him. One and then another of his men fell. Lanna's courage was instilling more confidence in some of the men who had been guarding the bank, and they quickly began to fire their own rifles at the outlaws, disregarding their own safety.

Sloan saw that he was going to lose more of his men if they stayed and fought on. Lanna was still shooting at him. But she was firing wildly now, not taking her time, and her rifle was soon empty.

Before she could reload, Coleman rode by her and stuck his pistol in her face. He made her get on a horse that was without a rider, and he ushered her out of town.

Sloan followed with the rest of the gang, less five men who had been shot and were lying in the street. The new bank was on fire, and the town had suffered the loss of a number of its citizens. Everything wasn't quite the way he wanted it, but he did have Lanna Mitchell.

It was one of the passengers who yelled and pointed out the window. Lassiter turned and looked back toward town, where a column of smoke was rising into the air. It appeared as if half of Glitter Creek was on fire.

The driver stopped the stage, and Lassiter quickly untied his sorrel stallion and got on.

"You take the shotgun with you!" Lassiter yelled up at the driver. "I doubt if you'll run into road agents, though. It looks like all of Sloan's gang are back in Glitter Creek. I hope something is left of it when I get there."

Lassiter rode hard back along the new road toward town. He was glad the wheel had needed repairs and they had gotten a late start, otherwise they would have been a long ways down the road. As it was, he would be getting into town too late to do much good. There was a lot of smoke rising above the trees.

By the time Lassiter reached Glitter Creek, a new doctor was treating the wounded, and the townspeople were trying to put out the fire at the new bank. Lassiter found the doctor kneeling over Harold Mitchell.

"How is he?" Lassiter asked.

"He's lucky," the doctor said. "The bullet only grazed his scalp. He's got a nasty knot on his head from falling into the wheel of this wagon, but he'll recover fast. Everyone thought he'd been killed."

Lassiter breathed a sigh of relief. But his relief suddenly changed to concern.

"Where's Lanna?" he asked the doctor.

"She's been taken hostage by Sloan and his men," the doctor said. "They rode out with her about a half-hour before you got here."

The doctor went on to tell Lassiter that Lanna had saved Glitter Creek with her rifle. The town was lucky there hadn't been more of its citizens killed or wounded. Due to Lanna's quick thinking and her use of the rifle, the town had literally been saved from total destruction. They had gotten to the new bank, but the rest of the town was still intact.

"And when Harold Mitchell comes to and learns what's happened to her," the doctor said in conclusion, "I don't know how I'm going to keep him down."

"You do your best," Lassiter said. "I'll take some men and we'll get Lanna back."

Lassiter walked up the street to where the men were putting out the fire. It was well under control, and some of them were starting to stand back to rest. It was getting late in the afternoon, and Lassiter was worried about Lanna. He knew he had to move fast to keep something bad from happening to her.

Lassiter called a meeting of the town council in the street, and they quickly discussed what Sloan was most likely planning: He would certainly use Lanna Mitchell as a tool for taking over the town. To stop this, they would have to act immediately.

"We have no time to lose," Lassiter told them. "They're disorganized, and now is the time to go after them. They won't expect it."

The discussion was in favor of leaving right away. Lassiter knew that to take too many men would only slow them down. He needed a choice few and asked the younger men who weren't married if they would ride with him. Seven of them gladly volunteered.

"It's time we ride into Miner Canyon," one of them said.

While the men got their horses and guns together, Lassiter saw to it that everyone who wanted could remain at the hotel and await the news of what happened in Miner Canyon. Harold Mitchell was resting as comfortably as could be expected with Lanna now a hostage of Big Jack Sloan and his gang. He reluctantly agreed to let Lassiter handle it. He would wait with the others.

The seven men and Lassiter checked their guns and ammunition. It was twilight; the western sky was shot with crimson and the cool night air of the mountains was rolling down. They mounted up and headed out toward the high country above the town, realizing there might not be a sunrise for some of them.

The posse led by Lassiter numbered fewer men than the outlaws, but the element of surprise was in favor of Lassiter. Sloan and his men certainly wouldn't expect a night raid. The trails to Miner Canyon led through deep and rugged mountains that were hard to negotiate in the daylight. Traveling by moon and starlight was taking a dangerous risk.

As they traveled through the heavy timber, Lassiter worried about what might be happening to Lanna. A bunch of road agents living in the mountains would certainly be happy to share a woman with Lanna's beauty. The only thing that would be in her favor was the element of time—there was no time to use Lanna before taking over Glitter Creek. Afterward, maybe, but time now was on Lassiter's side. Sloan would have to have Glitter Creek and all its assets in his possession immediately or lose the opportunity forever.

Gil Driscoll certainly had shown his hand. He seemed not to be afraid of Harold Mitchell or the townspeople of Glitter Creek. He had done them wrong but seemed so confident of Sloan and his gang that he wasn't concerned about what might happen should Sloan be defeated.

With Lanna's plight spurring him on, Lassiter led the posse up the Mullen Road and toward the trail that would lead into the hideout. The dark of night was in his favor, and he knew it all depended on what happened between now and when the sun rose tomorrow.

Sloan rubbed his leg and tried to forget the pain. The hard ride into Glitter Creek and the even harder ride back to the stronghold had taken its toll on the healing process in his leg. In addition, Morrison had been killed in Glitter Creek by Lanna Mitchell's rifle.

Gil Driscoll was now on his way back down into town. He wanted to make an appearance and say he had been out of town and hadn't known about what had happened. Sloan was glad to be rid of him. There was a plan cooking in Sloan's head, and he didn't want Driscoll around to argue about it if Coleman started in.

But now Coleman and the others were tearing at Lanna Mitchell's dress. They wanted at her right now. They hadn't even been in the cabin five minutes, and they were forgetting what was most important. They were forgetting that they still had to take total control of Glitter Creek.

Sloan had told them back on the trail that they were to go directly back down into Glitter Creek and take it over, that Lassiter and the others wouldn't be expecting this. He had told them that when they got back to the cabin they would make torches out of lengths of pine wrapped with old rags and doused in axle grease. But they wanted instead to waste time with the girl— time they couldn't afford to lose.

"Stop it!" Sloan bellowed. "I told you that can wait. Get those torches made!"

"This won't take long," one of them said.

"I don't care," Sloan said. "Leave her be for now."

The men began to complain, but they moved away from Lanna and set to work outside the cabin. Only Coleman remained behind, and he was trying to kiss Lanna on the lips while she fought him.

"Coleman!" Sloan barked. "Did you hear me?"

Coleman turned and scowled. "There's enough of them working to make plenty of torches," he said.

"That's not the point," Sloan argued. "I ain't letting you at her if none of the rest of them have time. Now, get out there and help them."

Coleman wasn't through arguing. "Jack, I'm your right-hand man. They can do that work."

Sloan looked hard at Coleman. He felt as if he were looking at Macey once again—the same sort of thing, arguing and rebelling against what he was told. It didn't seem to matter what you did to get a gang to follow you, there was always somebody sneaking up to take you from behind.

"You ain't any better enough than the rest," Sloan told Coleman. "You ain't about to have her alone. Now, get out there like I told you."

Coleman started for the door. He was glaring at Sloan as he walked.

"Now I get it," he said. "You just want her for yourself."

"And what if I do?" Sloan asked.

Coleman grunted and measured Sloan up and down before he left. He came back momentarily to see if Sloan had moved over closer to Lanna. But Sloan was waiting for him.

"I'll take the girl and the others down to Glitter Creek and leave you here," Sloan warned Coleman. "I want you to make torches. Either that or stay behind and cook breakfast when we get back. Which is it?"

Angered, Coleman moved out of the doorway and into the night to help the others cut pine limbs for torches. When Coleman was gone, Sloan turned to Lanna. She was trying to keep her torn dress together as best she could.

Sloan could see she was worried that Coleman was right. She thought he was going to come over and take up where the others had left off.

"You afraid of me?" Sloan asked.

Lanna didn't answer. She could see he was still gritting his teeth against the pain in his leg. He had moved back and was leaning against one wall. His leg was giving him a lot of trouble.

"You can't win this," Lanna finally told him. "You know you can't."

"What makes you think not?" Sloan asked.

"You can't keep your men together," Lanna said. "I hate to say this, but being without a leg and having the other leg shot up badly makes you weak in their eyes. You might as well just leave the country while you're still alive."

Sloan glared at her and struggled to his one leg. The pain was tremendous, but his anger was what made him grab the crutch and hobble over to Lanna.

"I could have you right now!" he spat at her. "In fact, I think I will."

"Try it!" Lanna yelled. She pushed him with all her might, and he tumbled backward onto the floor.

Sloan cursed and reached for the crutch. He swung at her, but she dodged the blow. Sloan was pulling himself along the floor on his knee with the crutch, trying to corner Lanna, when Coleman and the rest of the gang appeared in the doorway.

"We're ready to go, Sloan," Coleman said, barely able to hide his laugh. "But we can wait. It looks like you might need more time with her."

Now all the men laughed. Sloan pulled himself to his feet, and everyone stopped laughing when they saw Sloan glaring at Coleman. Sloan even had his hand down on his pistol. But Coleman had his hand on his as well. The rest of the men stared at Sloan and Coleman, waiting for one or the other to make the first move.

19

Sloan and Coleman continued to stare at each other. Coleman started to grin.

"You go ahead and draw," he told Sloan. "I want this to be fair."

"You feel like dying, do you?" Sloan said. He seemed to have forgotten completely about his shot-up leg. He was leaning against the crutch with his gun hand loose beside his revolver.

"I won't be the one dying," Coleman said.

Sloan grunted. "I've got a surprise for you."

From outside came the sound of a horse and rider approaching. Sloan and Coleman eased up some. Whoever was coming was in a hurry, and they didn't stop until they were right to the cabin. Everyone turned as Gil Driscoll burst through the door.

"We've got big trouble," he said. "Lassiter is riding up here with a posse."

"What did you say?" Sloan asked.

"I passed them as I was headed down onto the new

road—Lassiter and seven men. I think I got into the trees before any of them saw me. I think I did."

Everyone started to talk at once. If Lassiter was coming up here at this time of night, that meant he was going to try and wipe them out. It essentially meant the plan to surprise Glitter Creek had backfired.

There wasn't any time to lose in making a decision on how to handle the situation. Now the tension in the room between Sloan and Coleman suddenly shifted to the coming confrontation with Lassiter and the men from Glitter Creek.

"Let's take positions outside," one of the gang suggested. "We can pick them off as they come in."

"Lassiter isn't that stupid," Sloan remarked. "He's got something up his sleeve."

"Maybe they will stop if we tell them we'll kill this girl," Coleman said.

"That don't get us Glitter Creek," Sloan said. "I want to be down in that town by tomorrow, and I want it to be mine. We'll just ride on down and beat Lassiter at his own game."

"But if we tell them we'll kill this girl, they'll let us do what we want," Coleman continued to argue.

"Don't count on it, not with Lassiter," Sloan said. "He's—"

"That's why we've got this girl," Coleman broke in. "We took her to use as a bargaining tool."

"Shut up and listen to me!" Sloan yelled. He pointed at Lanna. "I shot her pa down in Glitter Creek today. She don't care if she lives or dies now. She'll just tell Lassiter to let us have her. Then we kill her and Lassiter and the rest of them kill us. We'll be trapped here."

Coleman nodded. "I expect you're right."

"Besides, I don't need no girl to stop Lassiter," Sloan said, his voice rigid with anger. "You men are going to see something pretty soon. Something you won't forget. Now, put that girl on a horse, and let's go get them."

Lassiter could see the torches coming through the trees. They had been riding a solid three hours through the heavy timber and still had a long way to go to reach Sloan's stronghold, but it appeared that Sloan was coming down to Glitter Creek.

"What do you make of that?" one of the posse members asked Lassiter.

"It can't be anybody but Sloan and his men," Lassiter said. "Somehow they had to know we were coming."

"Remember when I said I saw Gil Driscoll riding up ahead of us through the trees?" the posse member said.

Lassiter nodded. "That's who warned them. Driscoll has been in with them for a long time."

The posse member breathed a deep sigh. "And nobody wanted to believe you," he said. "Now we're going to have trouble."

"No," Lassiter said. "They're the ones with the torches. We'll let them come to that open meadow just ahead." He pointed out to where the timber broke into the open.

Lassiter got the seven men together and discussed how they would go at the Sloan Gang. They would use an old cavalry maneuver of charging out in a broken line and working the enemy into a bad position. Lassiter showed the posse where there was a rock wall along one side of the creek, where Sloan and his gang would become trapped after the initial charge.

Lassiter told the posse it was important that they shoot straight and keep in mind where everyone was at, so they didn't end up shooting one another. The meadow was open and there was enough light to see for a good distance. There should be no reason why any of the posse should mistake one another for one of Sloan's men.

"You make it sound easy," one of the posse members told Lassiter.

"It's not all that hard," Lassiter said. "We charge out there and surprise them, and they'll become confused. If we work it right, we'll have them tight against those rocks, and they won't stand a chance."

"What about Lanna?" another one of them asked.

Lassiter nodded. "That's the only thing about all this that worries me. She will surely be tied to a horse. And if we just open fire, they won't think to do anything but defend themselves. That's when I intend to get to her and bring her away."

Now the posse was worried about shooting Lanna. Lassiter told them again to make sure they knew who they were shooting. Lanna would be easy to pick out from the rest of them. And she would be smart enough to get into cover as soon as the shooting started. Lassiter then pointed out that it might be her chance to escape the gang.

"You're dreaming now, aren't you, Mr. Lassiter?" one of the posse members asked.

"That's what the world was built on," Lassiter said. "But more to the point, we haven't got any choice. Let's go get them."

* * *

Sloan and his men rode down through the timber and came to the edge of an open meadow splashed with moonlight. Sloan's leg was bothering him, but he wasn't going to show that to anyone. He had Lanna Mitchell with him, holding the reins to her horse. He didn't want her getting away from him.

Before they rode out into the open meadow, Sloan stopped and thought a moment. The meadow was open and the creek bordered a rock cliff on one side. That meant restricted room to ride in if something happened. That sort of situation bothered Sloan a lot. But he really didn't have any other choice; there was not a good trail of any sort along the steep, timbered slopes on the other side of the meadow. They had to go straight across.

Before they started across, Sloan called Coleman over.

"Have everyone put out the torches now. There's plenty of light from here on down."

The torches were put out, but Sloan still did not feel right about everything. He wondered if there was some way they could go back around and through another draw.

"What the hell is the matter with you?" Coleman asked. "We're strong enough to stop anybody. Besides, if we waste any more time, we won't make it to Glitter Creek before daylight."

"Then take a couple of men and check out the other side of this meadow," Sloan said.

"What for?" Coleman asked.

"Because I said so!" Sloan growled.

"Well, I'm tired of taking orders from you," Coleman said. "We've wasted enough time as it is. I'm taking the men down to Glitter Creek, and you're welcome if you want to come."

Coleman started out across the meadow, and Sloan thought about yelling at him. But that wasn't going to do any good. Sloan drew his pistol, but the other men were already following Coleman, and they were in the way. Sloan finally put his pistol away and cursed. Then he followed behind, leading Lanna's horse along.

Sloan became even more angered at what was happening. Coleman was taking the men at a faster speed than he had been riding and was now out ahead of him. He couldn't ride that fast, not with his leg the way it was. And he had Lanna Mitchell to consider.

Coleman and the others were about halfway to the timber on the other side when Sloan saw a group of men on horseback emerge from the timber. They were riding across at them at full speed. There was no question it was Lassiter and the posse. And they had them dead to rights.

Lassiter was in the lead, and the men with him were yelling. It reminded Sloan of when he had fought Indians just after the end of the war. That same fear he had known then came back up, and he turned his horse around.

There was a lot of confusion as Coleman and the others tried to get their guns ready. But the gunfighter, Lassiter, was among them with the posse, and though the posse was smaller, they shot unmercifully. Sloan could see that it was going to go very bad for his gang.

Sloan began to move, pulling on Lanna's horse. He could see what Lassiter was doing. Lassiter and the posse were sweeping around them in a semicircle, pinning them up against the rock cliff behind the creek.

Sloan's men fell left and right, while Sloan worked

his way back along the creek with Lanna Mitchell tied on the horse. Coleman and two of the gang managed to get back to Sloan somehow, and Sloan could hear them shouting, wondering what to do. Coleman seemed crazed, yelling that Lassiter was gunning them all down and that they had to do something.

"Get yourself together!" Sloan told Coleman. "Let the others try and fight them off. Our only chance now is to make a stand back at the cabin. We'll hold the girl there."

"Why not use her as a hostage here?" Coleman asked.

"There's too much confusion," Sloan said. "We can't stop them now."

Coleman was still acting confused. He was turning his horse in circles, yelling about going after Lassiter. The two other gang members were coming up with Sloan. They wanted no more of the fight.

"I said let's go!" Sloan yelled at Coleman. "We'll have to fight from the cabin!"

Coleman finally rode up. His breath was coming in short gasps.

"You want to die?" Sloan yelled at him.

"No!" Coleman yelled.

"Then let's go," Sloan said. "We'll use the girl as bait once we get to the cabin. Then, when Lassiter comes for her, we'll shoot them both."

20

LASSITER AND THE POSSE got down from their horses and took cover in the trees along the river. The Sloan Gang—or most of them—were pinned against the cliff and were shooting through the light of the moon, their rifles and pistols making long streaks of fire.

Lassiter was now looking to where he had noticed two of his men go down. They were at the far end, and now Sloan had Lanna and he was getting away, with Coleman and what appeared to be two other men. But the fighting was too thick for Lassiter to be able to move out and get his sorrel stallion. They would have to finish the remainder of the gang first.

While the others fired at the Sloan Gang, Lassiter began to think of a way to end it faster. He had no time to lose if he intended to catch up to Sloan and the others before they got back to their stronghold. Once they reached the cabin, his efforts to save Lanna would be useless.

Lassiter ran across the creek under a hail of gunfire and took position in the rocks adjacent to the Sloan

Gang members. When they turned to keep Lassiter from firing at them, they got shot at by the members of the posse. They were in a crossfire with no way out.

It was over quickly. Lassiter's rifle brought down three men, and then the others surrendered. They stood up and crossed the creek with their hands over their heads. There were just two gang members left alive, and one other man who had been worse on Glitter Creek than any of Sloan's other men. It was Gil Driscoll.

"Look who we've got here," Lassiter said.

Driscoll had his head down. He wouldn't look up for anybody.

"Take them down into town," Lassiter told the posse members. "I'm going up after Lanna."

Lassiter quickly jumped on the sorrel stallion and rode off into the night, hoping against the odds that Lanna was still all right.

The dawn light was breaking over the mountains as Lassiter crossed over the pass and down into Miner Canyon. He was not far from the outlaw stronghold now, but the shadows were still deep and riding was treacherous. He urged the sorrel stallion onward. He had to reach Sloan and the others before they got to the cabin.

The trail down into the bottom was steep, and Lassiter let the stallion pick his way as he alternated from full-out running through the meadows to an easier lope over steeper terrain. The stallion was used to the mountains, and Lassiter knew he had the edge in catching up with Sloan and his men, who were slowed down considerably by Lanna.

He wondered how close to despair she was at this

point. Her father had been shot, and it was likely that she thought he had been killed by the bullet. Now she was a captive of Sloan and the others. There was no telling what had happened to her and if she even cared about living at this point.

But the more Lassiter thought about it, the more he began to believe that Lanna wouldn't quit. She would likely be feeling pretty bad, but she wouldn't quit. She wouldn't let herself get to the point where she didn't care about living any longer.

It worried him now to consider what might happen to her if he pressed Sloan and the other three too tightly. Already most of the gang had been shot down either in town during the raid or up in the rocks that bordered the creek. Sloan wouldn't figure he had anything to lose by killing Lanna now—not unless he thought he could save his own hide by using her to barter with.

Lassiter was sure now that his best bet was to get to Sloan and the other three before they reached the cabin. Once in the cabin, Sloan could use her much more effectively than out in the open. If he shot her, then he knew his chances of survival were next to none.

As the sun began to rise, Lassiter found himself in an open meadow. The cabin was now less than a mile away. Lassiter kicked the stallion into a run. Right at the edge of a small meadow he almost ran directly into Sloan and his men. He saw Lanna look back on her horse, her eyes bulging. And he heard the voice of Big Jack Sloan just ahead of him. He was yelling at his men to get their horses moving.

Lassiter drew one of his pistols and charged ahead.

He could hear Lanna yelling over the voices of Sloan and his men. She was screaming at him to watch out.

Lassiter turned his stallion as two of Sloan's men turned their horses back and charged through the trees at him. They had their own horses running all out toward Lassiter and could not pull up in time before they realized they were riding right into Lassiter's twin .44s.

One of the outlaws shot wildly at Lassiter as he tried to turn his horse. But Lassiter was shooting with both pistols, a rein in each hand. The blast from Lassiter's guns was loud in the meadow, and the outlaw yelled and toppled from his horse.

The other outlaw was now turned on his horse, coming back at a different angle toward Lassiter. Lassiter held the stallion up and turned sideways to the oncoming outlaw. He thumbed three successive shots with his left hand that sprayed the outlaw up his right side, sending him off the other side of his horse and into a heap on the ground.

Lassiter realized he had no time to lose now and turned the stallion after Sloan and the other outlaw. He pressed hard, knowing he had this one last chance to catch them before they reached the cabin. This was the time to stop them, as there was no way they would kill Lanna as long as they thought there was a chance they could use her.

Lassiter caught up to them just as they were reaching the cabin. Coleman was riding in the lead while Sloan rode just behind him, holding the reins to Lanna's horse. Lanna was sitting in the saddle with her hands tied onto the saddle horn in front of her. She was working to pull the ropes loose.

Lassiter again charged forward with his pistols

drawn. He could see that Sloan wasn't riding all that well and was having trouble even staying in the saddle. For this reason he chose Coleman to go after.

It was important now to get up with Coleman and shoot him out of the saddle. Sloan could wait until later. Lassiter was aware that he would have to reload after just a few shots. But those few shots could make the difference.

But it wasn't Coleman that suddenly initiated the turn in the fight. Sloan threw the crutch off the saddle and released the reins to Lanna's horse. Then he pulled his pistol and turned the horse he was riding and spurred it hard.

The sudden jerk forward threw Sloan off balance, and with one leg missing and the other nearly useless, he tumbled backward off the horse and thudded to the ground. His pistol flew out into the grass, and his horse stormed past Lassiter as fast as it could run.

Sloan tried to regain his senses. The fall had left him badly dazed. Lassiter began yelling to Lanna to just get off her horse and run back toward him, but she was still struggling to get the ropes that held her hands off the saddle horn.

Suddenly Coleman was turning his horse around. He pulled his pistol and began firing at Lanna. Lassiter dismounted and pulled his Winchester from its scabbard. One of Coleman's bullets struck Lanna's horse, and it fell heavily to the ground.

Lanna had her leg free of the fall and the jolt twisted the ropes off the saddle horn, nearly pulling her arms from their sockets. She tumbled forward to the ground, dazed by the pain. Coleman, sensing the ease with which he could now kill Lanna, whooped and urged his horse into a faster run.

Lanna came to her feet and began to stumble forward into a run. Lassiter was waving his arm in a downward motion to Lanna.

"Get down!" he yelled repeatedly. "Get down!"

Lanna finally understood what he meant when she heard the firing behind her and felt the hot touch of a bullet against one of her legs. She dived into the fresh grass of the meadow and remained there while Lassiter pulled back the hammer of his Winchester.

Coleman was crazed for blood and he was nearly upon Lanna, his pistol again aimed at her. Lassiter had to shoot quickly now. He raised the rifle to his shoulder and fired. The bullet struck Coleman square in the stomach, and he doubled over. But he was strong enough to hold himself in the saddle, and he came ahead past Lanna toward Lassiter.

After levering another cartridge into the barrel, Lassiter rolled to one side as the wounded Coleman came by shooting. His aim was poor as the wound in his stomach held him doubled over. But he was so close that Lassiter could hear the bullets sing past him into the grass.

Lassiter again came to one knee as Coleman managed to turn his horse and charge back. There was no need to hurry this time, and Lassiter placed a bullet squarely into Coleman's chest, knocking him into a backward somersault off the horse and into the grass. He bounced once with the momentum of his fall and lay still.

Lassiter could see Lanna now running toward him across the meadow. Sloan had managed to find his crutch and make it to his feet. He was hobbling as fast as he could toward the cabin, intent on making his last stand from there.

Lanna made it to Lassiter's side, and he took her into his arms.

"I'm so glad you're here," Lanna told him. She was crying. "But it doesn't help my father. I'm afraid he's dead."

"No, he's alive and resting well," Lassiter told her. "The bullet just grazed him is all. He hit his head in the fall and that's what knocked him out."

"Oh, thank God!" Lanna cried. "I was sick with the thought he had been killed. I didn't care at first if anyone came up to help me."

"Did they hurt you in any way?" Lassiter asked. He noted that her dress was torn badly.

"They wanted to but Sloan made them stop," she said. "He wanted to get back down into town and finish what he'd started. I guess I owe him something."

"Don't worry, Lanna," Lassiter said. "He wasn't doing it out of charity. There's no telling what would have happened if they'd taken over the town."

"I didn't think I would ever get out of this," she said.

"Well, it's over now," Lassiter told her. "All but Sloan."

21

Lassiter told Lanna to stay behind him and get ready to drop to the ground if he told her to. Then he began to move forward cautiously against the enraged Sloan, who was by now almost to the cabin. To stop Sloan, Lassiter would have to shoot him in the back. But there was no need to even confront Sloan, for once he was inside the cabin, he was trapped.

"Don't go in the cabin!" Lassiter yelled. "There's no way you can come out of there alive!"

Sloan didn't bother to answer. He was working harder now to get inside, lunging on his shot-up leg, confident that when he reached the inside of the cabin he would become invincible. Lassiter saw him run into the cabin and slam the door. In a few moments, Lassiter realized, Sloan would have a rifle aimed out one of the windows and begin firing.

Lassiter pointed to where one of the dead outlaws lay.

"Take his rifle," Lassiter told Lanna. "You're going to need it before long."

Lanna hurried to pick up the rifle. Sloan was already shooting out one of the windows, and Lanna and Lassiter both moved into the trees for cover. They moved around to where they faced the front door, remaining behind the thick growth of timber.

"Sloan, don't be a fool!" Lassiter yelled. "You don't have to end it this way."

Sloan didn't bother to say anything. He kept firing his rifle repeatedly, caring little where the bullets went, hoping one of them would strike Lassiter or Lanna. Finally Lassiter realized that it was useless to try and talk to Sloan. He was likely crazy by now, wanting to end things like he thought an outlaw should.

"I'm not going to spend any more time with him," Lassiter said. "You fire at the front while I move over to his horse. I'll see to it that he either comes out or never draws a breath again."

Lassiter took one torch each from Sloan's horse and from Lanna's horse and made his way around behind the cabin. He was at the very back, where there were no windows, and he yelled in to Sloan.

"I've got some torches here," Lassiter yelled in to Sloan. "Come on out."

"Forget it!" Sloan yelled.

"I'm giving you one more chance to get out of there!" Lassiter yelled. "Come out with your hands up, and you'll be taken to the territorial capital for trial."

"Go to hell, Lassiter!" Sloan yelled from within the cabin. He began to shoot wildly, hoping to get a bullet to go through the chinking in the cabin at Lassiter.

Lassiter moved back to avoid being hit by the fire. Then he made his last statement to Sloan.

"It's over, Sloan!" he yelled.

Lassiter then took the first torch and struck a match to it. He threw it onto the roof of the cabin, where it immediately spread across the logs. While Sloan was cursing and raving inside, Lassiter then took the second torch, lit it, and tossed it through one of the windows that Sloan had broken out. Then Lassiter ran back through the trees to join Lanna.

Lassiter and Lanna watched together as the fire spread throughout the cabin. Lassiter watched the door. Still there was no Sloan, and it seemed impossible that Sloan would still be alive inside.

"He can't possibly be alive yet," Lassiter remarked.

"I thought I heard a muffled shot not long ago," Lanna said. "I heard it while you were running back through the trees."

Lassiter nodded. "Let's get you back down to town so your father won't be worried about you."

Lassiter rode with Lanna, both in a hurry to make it down into Glitter Creek so Lanna's father could see that she was fine. They talked of Glitter Creek's future. There was going to be a tremendous boom in the town now that the threat of road agents was gone. Lanna was hoping that Lassiter could be a part of it.

"I know you will want to be moving on now," she said. "But you know how I feel about you."

Lassiter nodded. "I've gotten fond of you, myself. But there's no good can come of it."

"Why not?" Lanna wanted to know. "You could

become the town marshal and there would always be me to take care of you.''

"You couldn't stand what would happen if I stayed on and became a marshal,'' Lassiter said. "Gunfighters follow me wherever I go. You would spend every day wondering if I was going to be killed or not. I told you, it wasn't a good idea that we see each other too much. I can't live with any woman, no matter what.''

"Times will change,'' Lanna argued. "The day will come when outlaws will cease to be.''

Lassiter chuckled. "Lanna, you know better than that. As long as there is gold and riches to build power for men, there will always be outlaws who will get it any way they can. That will never stop.''

"But no one has ever beaten you,'' Lanna said. "That won't change, either.''

"It's hard to hit a moving target,'' Lassiter pointed out. "Especially one that moves as often as I do. If I stay in one place too long, word gets around. That wouldn't be fair to you or to your father, or to the citizens of Glitter Creek, for that matter. They don't want blood in the streets; they've seen enough of that.''

They rode down past the cliff of rocks where the road agents had made their stand. At the edge of the meadow was a giant pine with large branches that reached out from the massive trunk. Hanging from two of the large branches were the two outlaws who had been with Driscoll. But Driscoll wasn't with them.

The two outlaws were turning slowly, their feet moving from side to side in the morning breeze. Lanna turned away from the sight.

"Where do you suppose Driscoll is?'' she asked Lassiter. "Do you think he got away somehow?''

"I hope not," Lassiter said. "He's a lot of trouble."

It was late morning by the time Lassiter and Lanna got into Glitter Creek. They could see a number of people gathered around the bank that had once belonged to Gil Driscoll. They were tearing it down and piling the lumber up for use elsewhere. It was being done under the direction of Lanna's father, who wore a bandage around his head.

Lanna jumped down from her horse and ran into her father's arms. Then Lassiter got down from the saddle, and Harold Mitchell took his hand.

"It seems we've been through this before," Harold Mitchell told Lassiter. "It's getting to be a common thing, you saving my daughter's life and bringing her back to me."

"This will be the last time I have to do that," Lassiter said. "There is no more Big Jack Sloan, nor is there anything left of his gang. But we don't know what happened to Driscoll."

"I can show you what happened to him if you'd like," Harold Mitchell said. He turned to Lanna. "You might not want to see this."

"If it's what I'm thinking," she said, "I've already seen two men who died that way."

Harold Mitchell took Lanna and Lassiter to the creek at the edge of town. There, hanging from a large tree, was the body of Gil Driscoll. His suit was rumpled and his pants were wet, and his banking days were over.

Neither Lassiter nor Lanna cared to linger near the creek, and they followed Lanna's father back up into town. The townspeople were all waiting for them, cheering Lassiter and Lanna. They all began to walk back up to the hotel, where Harold Mitchell was putting on a celebration for the rebirth of Glitter Creek. Mitchell gave Lanna another hug and kiss before he started up with the others.

"I'll see you and Lassiter up there in a little while," he said.

Lassiter stayed behind with Lanna, and they watched the people make their way to the hotel. It was going to be a fine celebration.

"I know you can't stay," Lanna said. "You already told me the reasons why. But I want to ask you just one more time to reconsider."

"It's just not me to stay in one place too long," Lassiter said. "There never was a finer woman than you. But I've got to be moving on."

"Lassiter, I will always think of you," Lanna said. "I will never forget you."

She kissed him, holding back tears, and they walked up through the trees to where the people were gathering at the hotel.

"I'll say good-bye to your father," Lassiter told Lanna.

Harold Mitchell noticed Lassiter and Lanna and walked out to talk. He could tell that Lassiter was getting ready to leave.

"That about settles it here," Lassiter said to him. "You have a new town and a new beginning. Glitter Creek should do very well."

"I know I'm speaking on behalf of everyone when I say I wish you would stay on," Mitchell said.

Lassiter threw the reins over the sorrel stallion's neck. "There are a lot of trails waiting for me out there," he said. "I've got to find them."

Lassiter then mounted and tipped his hat as he

turned the stallion. There were a number of townspeople who bid him good-bye as he started down the street. Lassiter rode from Glitter Creek while Lanna and her father waved and the sounds of the wind called him from the top of the ridge high on the Mullen Road.